In the Light of Men

# In the Light of Men

## Sam Desmond

NOBLE HOUND
PUBLISHING

IN THE LIGHT OF MEN
Copyright © 2025 Sam Desmond

All rights reserved. No part of this book may be reproduced
(except for inclusion in reviews), disseminated or utilized in
any form or by any means, electronic or mechanical, including
photocopying, recording, or in any information storage and
retrieval system, or the Internet/World Wide Web without written
permission from the author or publisher.

This book is a work of fiction. Names, characters, places, and
incidences are the product of the author's imagination. Any
resemblance to persons living or dead, actual events, companies,
or settings is purely coincidental.

Published by Noble Hound Publishing
FIRST EDITION

Book Cover and Interior Design by VMC Art & Design LLC
Cover and Interior Art by Emma Worth

ISBN: 979-8-9921152-1-5

Published in the United States of America

For my everything, (SD)²

# IN THE RESERVATION

Last night, I visited a storybook
  One I had lived in, but never read before

I couldn't go before,
  I didn't believe keys were made of air

For once I danced and felt the world,
  but lay without an answer

The gears calmed—the ones that never stopped,
  never oiled, never listened to themselves crack

The gears didn't break,
  they broke open and let the snowflakes
  cover the trail

The voices carried me to bed
The lamentations turned the sorrow into whimsy

I slept without ruminations torturing my thoughts
I awoke to sunlight beckoning my words

# The Carel Dispatch

## ONE TOWN, INFINITE COMMUNITY

**By Belén Stratton-Delaney**

For the past ten years, I have had the privilege of covering events in the bucolic Carel community.

What can only be described as a place that exists in the nostalgic collective of small towns captured in the cinema of the 1950s, Carel is near utopian in its blend of historical stock and contemporary appeal.

With landmark estates like Stratton Manor, beautifully and lovingly maintained by the recently renewed Carel Heritage Association, there is a hometown "Downton Abbey" that sports a working vineyard for cool summer nights with family (including dogs!).

But unlike other places that fall under the weight of their historical significance, Carel is constantly looking to preserve its proud, innovative, and stellar placement through community enhancements and strengthening of community ties.

Last winter, the Carel residents voted overwhelmingly (2 to 1) to allow a county-run women's psychiatric center at Stratton Manor— because that is the key tenet of "Spectre Spirit": to do what's best for the future generations of the community.

# In the Light of Men

Carel boasts one of the most active and involved Chambers of Commerce, which functions more like the co-operative Smurfs than a business organization.

Every company is homegrown in spirit and supportive of school and community projects. The Carel Opera House, which dates back to the Gilded Age, typically has sold-out shows for its four-show fall and spring seasons. Although it has never been confirmed, rumor has it that Marlon Brando graced the Carel Opera House's stage when he worked on the Fire Island Ferries as a teenager.

Local restaurants like Sullivan's, The Stage Coach, and Paula's Pub often sponsor community fundraising events that each easily have a dozen raffle baskets donated by other Chamber members. Thermo-Dynamic, Chiffon Suite, and Carel Horticulture lead the Beautification Committee's famed hanging planters initiative each year.

Local charities and civic groups like the Jack McCoy Foundation, Carel Civic Coalition, and FEED have long-reaching networks to identify and support down-on-their-luck Spectres in need of everything from basic school supplies to oil tank payments.

For ten years, I have gleefully written about pancake breakfasts, new businesses, three state championships for the varsity Spectres football team, both budding and established artists, and heartwarming stories like the woman who lived her 100 years in Carel.

Seeing Grand Avenue transform from a dirt road to the Goliath it is today, she saw Carel grow but always stay true to its sense of hometown pride.

As beautiful to run outside along the Great South Bay, if not more, than when I used to jog by the Jackie O reservoir when we lived in Spanish Harlem.

As a writer, I couldn't have asked for a more generous and inspiring muse than Carel: a town that stands for and delivers on the American dream.

# Part 1

# The Statesman

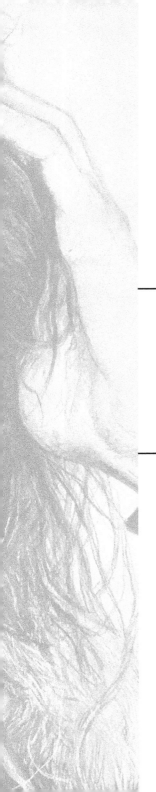

# FIRST ACT

# MAN FROM ATLANTIS

Please pretend you're not that perfect
There is no chance with the
gaping wound between us

I've gazed into your world and
offered to sell my soul for admission
only to find there was no market

My soul could not pass,
forced to look in as time celebrated

I've tried to swim to your world
I didn't drown
But I sank before the coast

I'm made of the same elements that make you shine
But I'm not the right tone
Even if you approve

You'll fight for us and combat the
    mortgage for my soul

But I'll have to surrender before the
    first try

# SECOND ACT

Part 1 | Act 2

# The Carel Dispatch

## WOMEN'S PSYCHIATRIC CENTER OPENS IN HISTORICAL HOME

### 'HUMANE TREATMENT' TOUTED BY LOCAL ACTIVIST

**BY BELÉN STRATTON DELANEY**

On July 14, 2015, The Eudora Stratton Therapeutic Center for Women opened in the Stratton Manor in Carel.

The initiative for the women's psychiatric facility was spearheaded by Carel's Assembly Legislature Representative, Carter Dixon, who secured over $6 million in state funding from the Department of Mental Health.

"There has been a lack of capable and inviting facilities to help with mental illness," said Dixon.

Eudora Stratton, the 102-year-old descendant of Carel founding father Hiram Stratton, who commissioned Stratton Manor in 1720, was present for the opening ceremony.

Stratton, who famously led a life of intrigue and self-described "excess" was hospitalized multiple times in her five marriages for what was then referred to as "hysteria."

After painful treatments, including radiation for her uterus to bring on early menopause, Stratton became a champion of the humane treatment of psychiatric patients.

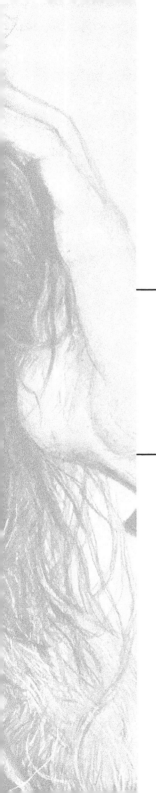

# THIRD ACT

Part I | Act 3

SHE WALKED INTO THE CHURCH LATE. ABOUT five past nine, but it was a weekday Mass, so she expected more leniency. The parishioners were mostly pensioners, probably playing catch-up with their clemency like they did with their 401k payments during their last five years in the workforce. She scanned both sides of the aisle to find him oddly enough sitting on the left. With his hair graying only on the sides, he was the youngest person she could spot. She walked up to his pew and put her hand on his right shoulder. He seemed surprised but didn't pull away instantly as he normally did. He looked up and smiled at her. A type of forced politeness, but she saw (or wanted to see) a genuine appreciation that she came.

It had been almost ten years since she last went to Mass. Most likely an Easter or a Christmas she couldn't get out of with her family. Sure, there was the baptism or wedding she had to attend, but those didn't count the same as non-sacrament Mass. And a weekday mass— she hadn't gone to one of those since Catholic grammar school.

But church meant a lot to *him*. She liked to say she was an atheist but knew it wasn't true. No one raised Catholic ever got the Church fully out of their system.

## SAM DESMOND

Especially as an artist, who could resist the calling of the stained glass, the carved wood ceilings? The recitation of prayers and methodology was like the joy of breaking up a particularly rocky eight ball with a dollar and a quarter. Both processes made you fall in love with the Eucharist.

He had said to her she should "come back." Almost like how her Irish-Catholic father denied she was actually an atheist, "because she wasn't raised that way." She wondered if her father had come back to church when he went through a depression all those years ago. Did all middle-aged white men come back to God when their worlds fell apart?

He stepped out of the pew to let her in to sit. The kneeler was already down.

"I can't believe you came."

She put her right hand on top of his left and gave it a reassuring but maternal squeeze, "Of course."

The music started, and they both stopped talking to focus on the altar as naughty children chiding themselves for disrupting Mass. They both grabbed a hymnal. She wondered if he was the type to sing aloud or silently mouth the words. He was too broken to even do the latter. She thought ahead to parts of the Mass when they would be permitted to touch, wondering if he would.

There was the part where they said the "Our Father," where there would be a chance to hold hands. But not every parish had done it that way. Then, of course the "Peace Be With You" part. They were too close to just shake hands. Would he kiss her on the cheek or just hug her for it? She sat down and crossed her legs at the ankle

# In the Light of Men

because Sister Abruzzo had said "only a puttana crosses their legs at the knee." He kept his head down most of the time with a crestfallen expression that never let up, even when their eyes met.

She wanted to be what church was for him. She wanted to be a break in his never-ending sadness. She had always wanted to be an older man's beautiful, youthful silver lining. Instead, she had turned into another source of stress for him. She kept a screenshot of the text he had sent her months ago: "I need a breather from our friendship. You're right. You do add stress to my life. I'm sorry, we'll talk soon." It had devastated her to read it. She overanalyzed every part of it. Why did he always have to limit her being just a friend? Was he really not attracted to her? Why did he say he needed a breather and then add in some corporate throwaway line like, 'talk soon'? They had talked every day for months, and leading up to it, she had felt his responses had grown more obligatory—he would just answer a question, never expanding or lengthening the conversation. But instead of giving him space then, she pushed on and brought him to the point he had to be cruel.

Even now, her presence was probably causing him undue stress. But she couldn't stay away from him. She hadn't been able to for over a year now. She had thought, or hoped, he felt marginally the same way. Amidst all the pain in his life, seeing "Good morning, handsome ;)" as the first text of his endlessly busy days would make him smile. He had said she was a "great friend." That he "cherished" her. They had regularly said "love you" and

Part I | Act 3    19

SAM DESMOND

"love you, too." Granted, she always said the first part. On text anyway. He always said it first in person or on the phone. She had hoped he would see all the horrible events of the past few months as a way to bring them together.

He always said he just wanted to "know God's plan" because he couldn't figure out what awful thing he had done to deserve all the loss and betrayal he was being subjected to. She wanted to say His plan was her. It was them. He once said, "God brought you to me. I know He did. He sent you to me." She thought, in retrospect, it was wrong to have responded with, "Thanks for magical negro'ing my existence!" Maybe she should have fed the seed instead of scoffing at it. Maybe he felt scorned. Maybe, again, he was just being polite. She just wanted him to tell her. No, she wanted him to see her the way she wanted to be seen.

They stood, and she saw other parishioners grasp each other's hands. She offered her right hand to him, which he clasped lightly, to her disappointment. She started to chant the "Our Father," wondering why they didn't say the "Apostle's Creed" as she wanted to impress him with how well she knew it despite her decade-long absence from Catholicism. That somehow this would be a sign for him that they were meant to be together. He dropped her hand instantly as the prayer ended. She held back her tears and followed along in a hollow way. What was wrong with her? Why didn't he want her? What could she do to change that? She missed him so much. She missed his words. She missed his undying nobility. He

20    Part i | Act 3

In the Light of Men

had the most beautiful compliments for her work. The first short story she ever showed him, he said, "I thought it was based on Marilyn Monroe, but then I thought no. No, it's Jackie Kennedy." He knew to say that before even knowing about her obsession with JFK. She felt his pain when she listened to Otis Redding. She wanted him because he had said "no" a million times.

"And peace be with you," the priest said.

They turned to each other. They both stood motionless.

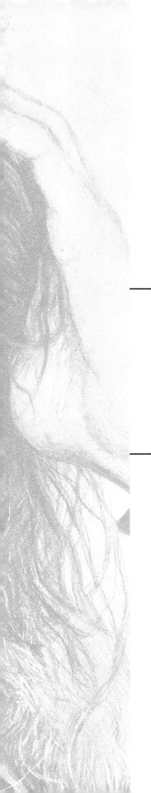

# FOURTH ACT

Part 1 | Act 4 23

# THE PERFECT DAY

There is a consensus on a beautiful day, but
What if sunlight hurts your perspective?
What if blue reminds you of a stolen, unrequited
lover's eyes?
What if your embrace is from a wool coat?
What if you need the snow festivities to divert
your ever-anxious mind?
What if barren trees remind you of potential?
What if flowers chide you with a reminder of
what you do not have?
Do not placate me with your smiling solaris
Grinning does only to point out the grind
Give me the might and power of nature to
overcome me, to help me shred the time

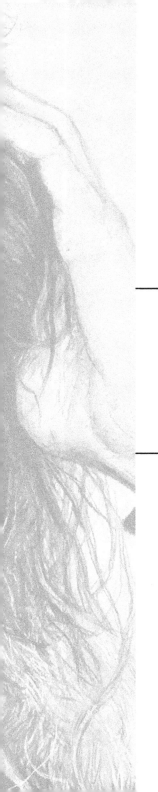

# FIFTH ACT

SHE LOOKED AT HIS NAME ON THE SIGN AT THE entrance to the psychiatric center. It made her happy to see it. She was sure, on some level, he had a narcissistic moment of glory seeing his name on a government sign. The grounds of Stratton Manor were truly beautiful, apt for convalescence, and with spring just awoken, it hadn't yet fulfilled the horticultural spectrum it was meant to. Since it was Easter Sunday, she felt like it should have been in full bloom. If nothing else, as a photo op for every J. Crew/L.L. Bean-clad family in the area. At least that would make him smile to see it being used and shared by the community.

Did he still love the community after what had happened? His wife being so forgotten that she claimed she had a right to be driven into the arms of another. Some loser who had the time to sit around and text bullshit because he didn't have an important job. And what a perverted sense of sisterhood that assured his wife she was right to do what she did. But, now Belén had the opportunity to have him in her world for a while because of it.

He pulled into the parking lot in the brash, American government-issued car of his. She was relieved he

SAM DESMOND

didn't pick it out himself but thought how much more upsetting it would be to see an elected official choose a luxury German or Japanese car. Ford, or Lincoln, was a good choice for him. American, but not as hick as Chevy. Jeeps weren't remotely American anymore, and Wranglers, the only Jeep of interest for someone who drove a restored Defender, were too much of a "little boy's toy" car. At least it was black.

He was wearing the pullover sweater that the local police had made up for him with his name. He loved wearing that. It was power beyond a suit. He was so quintessentially all-American that he hardly seemed real. Little League and pancake breakfasts were more apt for his Sunday mornings than meeting with a friend committed to a psych ward with a dubious ulterior motive. On the other hand, he was also a politician and a conservative one at that, so maybe the only odd part of this meeting was that she wasn't an underage boy. But even that thought was Huffington Post-blasé. After directly espousing so many inclusive views, part of her thought he wasn't even really a conservative, but ran as a Republican because of the demographics of the constituency, like a Bloomberg Republican of sorts. Her politically fringe and decidedly leftist friends also delighted in this imagined dalliance because "conservative" was the new gross, avante-garde. "I just want to suck Marco Rubio dry," her best, obviously gay, friend Chaim told her after she described Carter to him.

He waved to her from the car as he finished up a

In the Light of Men

phone call. He was always finishing calls or writing back text messages and emails. Probably part of that "he didn't put me first" caterwauling his wife cited as a reason for having an affair and putting their kids through this. But it was all about results. All about bettering a community. Why would you be selfish enough to put yourself ahead of that? But Belén wasn't a mother, so her thoughts were probably moot. There was probably a whole litany of dismissive transgressions he committed that she would never understand.

But the bottom line was his wife fucked somebody else—someone in the immediate circle—she cheated on the kids. Belén had eschewed motherhood before she was even a woman—or did she still count as only a girl because she was sans rugrats?—because of this binding pressure to always make good choices. His wife had to be a selfish cunt. There was no other explanation.

He finally put his phone away. To her slight dismay, in his pocket instead of leaving it in the car. She loved the way he walked. Jaunty, confident. Only privileged, (premium, not basic) white men walked that way. That walk and head angle that so, "No, my opinion is how we're going to do things." It afforded him enough success to tack on a political seat on top of being a Vice President at a BeNeLux bank. Belén was surrounded by artists, writers, and creatives—people who thrived on diversity and others' willingness to accept individual, alternative strengths. He represented a world of fierce conformity and competition. But yet, he made her feel more accepted than her fellow comrades. Was it

Part I | Act 5 31

## SAM DESMOND

some latent high school need to be liked by an athlete? Probably. She was sure he played varsity something at that height and with those shoulders. If he liked her, it meant she was a rebel to the suburban dream, not an unwilling outcast.

And her choice not to be a mother was a choice, not a sentence for her shortcomings. He said to her once that he thought she'd be a great mother. But were all gentlemen programmed to speak that way? Her psychiatrist reminded her that her medication was Schedule B for pregnancy. Not that that was even the most severe of issues. How could she fend off the depression that inevitably came to her, even if unpredictably so? How would she ever not be dependent on someone else's steady income as an artist? She did begrudge his wife that—she was successful and probably made enough money as a finance exec or lawyer, but she could never remember which one—she was able to support their kids without him. Was she deifying him because she wouldn't have the same walkaway power his wife did?

He finally sat down across from her on a plastic, municipality-grade picnic bench underneath the bright white pergola in the front lawn of the manor.

"Hey buddy, how are you?" Buddy, the death knell of her courage to ever try anything with him.

"I'm ok. How are you handling the day so far?"

"It's so hard. It's our first holiday not really as a family, and it's stressing out everyone. I'm so not myself today."

"Where are you going?"

32    Part i  |  Act 5

## In the Light of Men

"My sister-in-law's..."

She took a second to take in the "Gone With the Wind"-era chivalry of what he just said to her. "Isn't that going to be awfully awkward? Do they know?" she asked, knowing that even if they didn't, she was sure his wife had already gotten her sister on her side.

He looked down, crestfallen. "Yes, everyone knows."

She wanted to ask to what extent everyone knew. "How are you such a gentleman through all this? You're really being generous in letting her have dignity."

"It's extremely difficult. I live day-to-day. I pray for strength and inner peace. But this has been a nightmare and the most painful experience of my life."

She reached across and cradled his hand. He didn't wince. "Well, the dating world is cruel and unforgiving to women in their late forties."

"It's awful for everyone."

"At least you can always grab a twenty-something piece of arm candy."

He gave a dry chuckle, "No, not my style. I want someone beautiful on the inside as well as the outside." *Did he just call me fat?* She had to wonder.

"Well... do you prefer blondes, brunettes, or redheads?"

"It doesn't matter to me..."

"Well then, how do I narrow down which one of my hot friends to set you up with?" *Please say you'd like me and not my hot friends...*

"I'm going to need some time." She felt ashamed at her shallow attempts to make him feel better. Men weren't supposed to have *this* depth of emotion. Not

SAM DESMOND

like this, anyway. They were supposed to want the next slice of majestically hot pussy without a thought of the ones they'd abandoned.

"I'm sorry. I'm just trying to make you feel better. You should at least date some leggy, gorgeous woman to annoy the hell out of your wife."

"Oh, trust me. I plan on it." *So once again, not me*, she lamented.

"Your kids will always remember what a gentleman you were during all this when they learn the truth."

"I just want my old life back. The life I had three months ago."

"But that was a façade. Do you really want to go back to a lie? Or do you want to live the lie just because it was easier than dealing with the truth?"

"No, you're right. It was a lie. But then that's still 20 years together, pissed away."

She didn't have an answer. She continued to stroke his hand with her thumb and gave a look of sympathetic devastation.

"I'm sorry, I gotta get going. She'll be back from taking the kids to the driving range soon, and I still need to get dressed for Easter."

She lamented that their closest touch was a handshake in church during the 'peace be with you' part.

"Same here."

They both got up, and he started walking towards his car.

"You really have become a dear friend to me. Thanks for everything."

# In the Light of Men

"Of course." She opened her arms for a hug. He leaned over and let out a dismal sigh.

# SIXTH ACT

Whaddup, slut?

It was Belén's best friend, Blair, texting.

Yeah, I wish. He's not here yet.

But he didn't say 'no,' right?

No, but he still could. He always does.

Yeah, on texts where it's very easy to screw someone over because it's obvious and unable to be twisted, that's how he found out his wife was screwing around on him, isn't it?

Well, technically, he just said 'phone records'—

Exactly. He's still in divorce limbo, so he won't be stupid enough to let her lawyers find him at fault.

Aa

Part I | Act 6

## SAM DESMOND

> You fucked a lawyer, and now you're a legal expert?

Hey, keep in mind it was your game plan that I followed to get my lawyer. You were the one who said to volunteer to run the social media for his firm and make it all about getting his vision out there.

> I also told you to play the happy mistress, and you got his wife to knock down his office door hunting for you!

Whatever! He wasn't happy. And why are you always so defensive of the wife?

> Because his wife didn't deserve that.

Oh please, yes she did. She had taken him for granted for years. Just like your competition did.

> She is not my competition—

Aa

# In the Light of Men

> Oh yes she is. That's why you keep reminding him of how selfish she acted so he can act selfishly. With you.

> Am I just not hot enough to pull this off? I should've waited until I lost more weight—

> Oh my God, stop it. No one wants to fuck someone who's a ball of insecurities. You're going to wind up cock-blocking yourself with the whiny teenager bullshit. If you weren't attractive to him, then why would he pay as much attention to you as he does?

> I don't know. He always calls me 'friend.'

> That's a politician thing.

> And he's said 'no' before.

Aa

Part I | Act 6     41

> Well, hun. He's officially separated now. Different setting, different rules.

> Why am I so obsessed with trying to fuck him? How pathetic am I? He keeps saying 'no,' and I keep trying. Shouldn't I have more respect for myself?

> Cause the dick's that good to you in your mind. It's a quest, you won't stop until you get it. Hopefully, he lives up to it.

> Ugh… why can't I be normal?

> 'Cause you're an artist, darling. You'll always want to fuck your muse.

> I really thought after writing about him as another Mike Bloomberg he'd have said 'yes.'

Aa

In the Light of Men

> Yeah… you always go so over the top. It's off-putting how you deify someone you want to fuck.

> I can't help it. I am certified crazy.

> And he's made it his political career to help crazies like you. It was meant to be. I'll call you tomorrow. Bye, sweetie.

Her phone rang. It was him. She let it go to voicemail.

Aa

Part 1 | Act 6   43

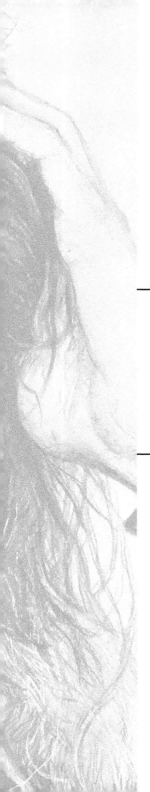

# FINAL ACT

## FIVE YEARS LATER

> OMG, yaaaaasssssss! You're right! We totally should bring snacks to the fascist ball!

Belén texted her best friend-now-editor, Blair.

> Right?! 'Cause the foods are only for the VIPs, we'll bring a whole bunch of snacks to eat during the night!

> This is legit the only time in six years of friendship that we'll be out like actual friends.

> I know, but that's so us.

> True. I love us. <3 <3

> What are you wearing?

> A dress. I felt so underdressed the first year I went.

Aa

Part I | Final Act    47

# SAM DESMOND

> Oh, I know, the fascists are well dressed.

Yeah, I know, all the rich men in suits.

> LOL, Carter always looks so fucking hot.

Total silver fox.

> You think he'll bring his wife?

I still can't believe they're back together.

> I know. Fuck her. She fucked a short, unemployed man.

When she had Carter!

Aa

# In the Light of Men

The fascists really knew how to decorate. It was the third year Belén had covered the Republican victory party at the Orange Grove. The red, white, and blue balloons and cinematic lighting made for the best front-page covers. And it worked out well because they were going to decimate the Democrats this year. All the campaign signs were curated throughout the large space and the stage just like some "Citizen Kane" party.

Blair was still cheering her personal victory of deciding to make their publisher reimburse her $2.50 parking fee.

They took a selfie, and Blair posted it with the caption, "Working for our money—we'll be here 'til midnight!"

"Gordon actually love reacted the post!" said Blair.

"Really? I feel like he's still upset he can't own us as slaves like his ancestors did."

"Right? He's like, 'why do these slaves keep asking for money!'"

"I feel bad I didn't bring snacks too, but I seriously thought I was going to stay on track this week after all the weight I gained during Halloween," Belén said.

"I know, me too! But it's Election night!"

"I know, it's journalist Superbowl. We should just enjoy ourselves. So what'd you bring?"

Blair opened up the mom cooler and displayed an array of snacks that only a mother of three under seven would have.

"Oh my God, you brought Bugles?!"

"Yes, and salami and mozzarella, and I brought chocolate for when we want dessert!"

"You're the best! I can't wait to start snacking on this!"

The DJ at the Republican victory party was always the best and cranked out late-'90s, early-2000s rap that was always thoroughly enjoyed by the crowd.

It made sense, despite surface differences, that rap of that era was exceptionally Republican in thought: make an empire and defend it with violence if need be. Face down, ass up. Did any man driving a luxury car now between the ages of 35 to 45 not imagine P. Diddy's "Can't Hold Us Down" playing as they rolled up?

"Oh my God, look, it's Carter!" Blair sat up and reached her arms out for a hug. "Oh fuck, he brought his wife."

Carter walked over, dashing as always, followed by his equally (and annoyingly) regal wife, who was also incredibly tall, statuesque, and had the jawline of cut marble. Whatever esthetician she used definitely made it look natural on her.

"How are you guys?" he asked earnestly between hugs. "You've met my wife, right?"

"We're Facebook friends! Belén, I love your posts. You lost so much weight, and you did it healthily. You look great!" his wife said to Belén in the middle of hugs.

"Thank you so much! You look amazing, too."

"Oh thanks! Wasn't sure how to dress, still tired from driving back from Colorado!"

"Oh that's right, where your daughter goes to school!

# In the Light of Men

Did she pledge a sorority? I heard BamaRush was a huge thing on TikTok. It's probably big in Colorado, too."

"She did her first year, but you know, the girls can get so feisty, so she didn't really want to do it again."

"Gotcha, you must be exhausted from the drive."

"Oh yeah, but my daughter had on this murder podcast that just kept me so intrigued!"

Belén's ears perked up as a serial killer enthusiast. "Oh my God, all I ever watch now is true crime!"

"YES! I don't get it, the bloodier, the better. After I finish listening to one, I'm always like, 'Should I watch puppies playing now?'"

"And all the ones where they murder their husbands?"

"YES! Have you watched 'Gone Girl'? I LOVE that movie!"

"Me too! And you could totally do that to Carter, he's an elected official."

His wife narrowed her eyes on him. "Oh my God, it'd be so easy!"

Carter was pulled aside by someone important-looking who pointed to the stage.

"We have to talk more about this!" His wife yelled as he took her hand.

"Shit, she's really hot," Blair lamented after they left.

"I know, but I think I actually like her!"

"I know, she seemed cool."

Belén texted Carter.

> Hey, you guys looked great last night. I got an awesome shot of you and your wife at the podium.

> > Oh really? That's great.

> You had the highest victory of any Republican. 66% of the vote.

Belén sent the podium photo.

> Look at that look of admiration and love on her face for you.

> > Yes, I love it.

Aa

52   Part I  |  Final Act

In the Light of Men

> So it did all work out in the end.

Is this the first time you've met her?

> Yeah, she's amazing. I may actually be more into her than you now.

I'm so glad you and my wife had a chance to connect.

Aa

Part I | Final Act

# Part 2

# The Academics

# FIRST ACT

Part 2 | Act 1    57

# The Carel Dispatch

# THE QUEEN AND DEAN

## REMEMBERING REAL-LIFE ROYALTY

**BY BELÉN STRATTON DELANEY**

Whenever something happens with the royal house of Windsor, all of England turns into a small town.

What I love most about covering our small town is exactly the spirit that is fueling the bittersweet celebration of a life well-lived in all corners of the United Kingdom right now—a sense of knowing someone through constancy, dependability, and a damn good duty to community.

Town historian Dean Stratton was a local royal to those who knew him and those who knew of him, living a life that served as a place-keeper for a long, trusted, and continuing history.

The first time I heard of Dean Stratton was with our good friend, power broker Realtor Nigel Whitby, when we were house hunting in the Carel area during the respite spring of 2013.

Searching for a home south of Montauk after the fury of Superstorm Sandy the previous fall, the luster of coastal living was somewhat diminished by the fresh cruelty of Mother Nature.

Part 2 | Act 1    59

## SAM DESMOND

But our anxiety was calmed when Nigel showed us a home on Snedecor Avenue that had been spared by the wrath of Sandy and had been on Dean's historical tour.

Nigel told us how Dean recounted how this perky little structure had withstood some of the most devastating storms of the century.

He spoke of Dean as the consummate, sagacious professor but also a man who inspired awe and further curiosity of the town's collective past.

When I first met Dean at a Carel Chamber of Commerce meeting a year later, after we settled into our dream cottage (lovingly plaqued with an English-countryside-inspired sign that read "Squirrel Cottage" that Dean loved), he lived up to the Ivy League-professor image I had of him in his smart bow tie and perfectly pressed pants.

*The Dispatch's* colorful publisher (whom I affectionately called Rupert á la media magnate, Rupert Murdoch) introduced us.

Dean, a veteran and heralded writer of *The Carel Dispatch*, welcomed me, a new, young voice on the paper.

When I expressed my apprehension about "being an outsider," he warmly offered, "Let the real stories of Carel guide you, and you'll always be a part of the town."

And that was Dean Stratton—-paradoxically intellectual and yet paternal with others.

The first article I ever worked on with Dean was about his family's ancestral home, Stratton Manor.

Abstractly, I knew the manor was built in colonial times, but not much else.

Dean invited me to his home, a smaller cottage on the property that was a perfectly preserved historical treasure that housed an impressive library, with all the warmth of a grandfather's grin.

I told him I wanted to make his ancestors more accessible to a contemporary audience, and he regaled me for two hours on

# In the Light of Men

the shenanigans of the young Roosevelts and Gillettes who often visited the Strattons until ultimately establishing summer homes of their own, until they were transformed into Edwardian Kardashians.

That was the magic of Dean's tireless work and joyful parallels——he preserved the beauty of the mythical appeal of history, but brought the enchantment of humanity of the central figures, much like Queen Elizabeth did with the royal family in a contemporary world that was finally asking for the sins of colonialism to be atoned.

Upon hearing of his passing in the fall of 2019, Carel was unhinged with mourning on social media.

Every post garnered hundreds of not just "likes" but "love" and "sad face" reactions to images of the ever-dapper Mr. Stratton at events around the towns.

The word that came up the most to describe Dean was "gentleman," and it couldn't be more apt for the great man who led his life as a discoverer, storyteller, and icon of the South Shore's treasured history.

Alas, whether it be Queen Elizabeth II, Dean Stratton, or a relative—be not sad for the passing, but celebratory of the legacy.

# SECOND ACT

Part 2 | Act 2    63

# The Carel Dispatch

# TEACHER'S COQUETTE

## THE MODERN WOMAN IN HISTORY

**BY BELÉN STRATTON DELANEY**

On the Scandalous Women tour at the preeminent Metropolitan Museum of Art, staid, state portraits become 17th and 18th-century versions of "selfies." With Professor Alex Snedecor, a native of Carel who still summers in the area while living on the Upper East Side of Manhattan, explaining the historical context of the paintings with his humorous approach, it's as if these were the "Twitter feeds" of the era's celebrities and statesmen.

An Ivy Leaguer as both student and staff member, Professor Snedecor has been leading lectures open to all with the Scandalous Women tour, where the gossip and fun of art history shed fresh light on the material.

While on Professor Snedecor's Scandalous Women tour at the Metropolitan Museum of Art, I went into full millennial mode, posting on Facebook literally (improper usage here) every two seconds because of the hilarity with which the formidable academic delivered his apex cocktail-party conversation knowledge on art history and the human condition.

My favorite post was on Pompeo Batoni's "Diana Stealing Cupid's Bow," where Professor Snedecor off-handedly reminded the diverse two-dozen-member tour group of how to maximize the appearance of one's breasts—whether for high art of the 18th century or a JCPenney intimate apparel sale—by raising your arms above your head.

Stuffier, more characteristically staid tour groups flanking us in the European paintings wing stared longingly as our guide had us in stitches in front of some of the Met's most revered paintings.

Entertaining and enthralling, Professor Snedecor has made academic accessibility the cornerstone of his teaching style by simply allowing art (all the way back to the classics, his specialty) to speak truthfully—whether that language be sex, intrigue, politics, or cattiness.

Even more effective and engaging than the "dream teachers" of "The Dead Poets Society" and "Dangerous Minds," Professor Snedecor is both cognizant and respectful of the need to connect modern audiences to what can appear to be a culture far removed.

"A large part of the popularity of the Scandalous Women tours is how much more contemporary women identify with the courtesans than they do the traditional wives of history. Today's women have more freedom as intellectual beings, consumers of fashion, and as lovers—that is paradoxically more in line with these 'kept' women."

As the founder of the Scandalous Art Tours (the parent company of Scandalous Women), Professor Snedecor is putting to use his extensive and nuanced knowledge of art and history, forged during his student days at Yale (B.A.) and Columbia (Ph.D.).

With his celebrated book, "The Beautiful Boys of Ancient Greece," Professor Snedecor is a foremost expert on the history of

# In the Light of Men

same-sex love (and as he shows on the Scandalous Women tour, a connoisseur of all naughty romantic entanglements, opposite-sex as well as same-sex).

"As Americans change their public-face views on homosexuality and marriage, it's important to acknowledge that some of these 'progressive' stances are actually harkening back to classical or traditional norms of older societies."

A travel enthusiast, Professor Snedecor's enterprising dream for Shady Ladies Tours is a series of multi-day European tours of museums. This will not be your great-grandmother's "Daisy Miller grand tour of Europe": Professor Snedecor envisions a sweeping series of lectures on the sexy secrets of high-brow collections by pointing (and poking fun) at the not-so-hidden homages to courtesans, on the model of the 8-day gay history tour of London and Paris.

The sly observation that the Metropolitan Museum of Art in New York contains a substantial number of portraits of mistresses, courtesans, and other steadily employed ladies of the night was the initial inspiration for Professor Snedecor's popular Scandalous Women tour and one he will undoubtedly expand to other bastions of the art world.

When asked if there are any courtesan-level role models today, Professor Snedecor said that Kim Kardashian regrettably does not come close to Grace Dalrymple Elliott. Instead, he cites Marlene Dietrich as the last of the great Scandalous Women, reflecting, "These women were able to blaze a trail at a time when women were barely allowed to hold candles. They resonate with contemporary women because as the world evolves to finally give women the rights and powers they have been entitled to lead full lives, these are the few women of the past who were able to command respect, love, and admiration, all while being self-aware of their beauty and charms."

# THIRD ACT

Part 2 | Act 3    69

# The Carel Dispatch

# 'TO DIE ALIVE' EXPLORES LIFE BETWEEN THE DAYS

## FIRE ISLAND ARTIST CAPTURES SEA AND SAND IN SOLILOQUY FASHION

### BY BELÉN STRATTON DELANEY

With the beach being a generous and common muse to photographers, it is rarely captured under its veil of solemnity at night, where the cool, mystic undertones of the moon replace the Technicolor haughtiness of the sun.

Carel native turned Fire Island photographer Huston Gillette, who captures brilliant, celestial bodies both at the horizon line and above, explores the vivacious life of Cherry Grove and The Pines after dark in his book, "To Wish For," recently published by Penguin.

The images are unabashedly erotic, but belie a sanctity in the ephemeral ecstasy of trysts in the Meat Rack, the woods that separate

# SAM DESMOND

Cherry Grove and The Pines, where late-night and anonymous love affairs take place between the denizens of the two beaches.

Gillette's models are wrapped in moments of pleasure and exploration but are always aware of the tentativeness that the cover of moonlight provides them. Even in photos where there is a group dynamic, there are overtones of a Goya scene, but always celebratory and introspective in the gaze given by the models.

Often fully in the nude, Gillette's models, whom he gathers through friendships and open calls, are harbingers of the sans vanitas movement that has a direct link to the Baroque period.

Shot in 35-mm film, with long exposures and highly staged subjects, Gillette does not direct his models to have specific facial expressions, but rather lets them have free rein after establishing an artistic relationship with them during the photoshoot.

"It's almost like they're giving me permission to hold still," said Gillette.

Asked what most intrigued him about the island at night, Gillette spoke of the "blue wash" that overcomes the beach from the moonlight.

As a youth in Carel, Gillette was a skilled sailing instructor who would often take the family boat out after everyone had gone to sleep and head over to Fire Island.

This put his early photoshoots between 10 p.m. and 12 a.m., which continues with his artwork today. Serendipitously with his teenage rebellion, that time at night is when the moonlight is at its most beautiful, before it becomes maddening.

A place of particular curiosity that has become a muse of Gillette's is the black, burnt wood that evokes the "mysteriousness" of the woods.

Five years ago, a fire burned a section of Sunken Forest and left behind a skeletal system of trees covered in noir nature.

# In the Light of Men

"I like the mystery of how it came to be, and I've known of people in our community who have spread the ashes of loved ones in these woods, especially during the height of the AIDS pandemic," said Gillette.

Central, but not all-encompassing, of Gillette's work is the gay culture of Fire Island's The Pines and Cherry Grove.

The Belvedere Hotel, "iconic of queer architecture," according to Gillette, is a welcome backdrop in much of the work featured in "To Wish For," with both interior and exterior shots.

The opening photo, where nude bodies take up artistic space on the roof of The Belvedere, is evocative of a neoclassical revival that beckons the viewer to be at one with both the male gaze and the male figure.

In interior shots of the hotel, multiple figures are arranged intimately, but always with a hesitancy before the true congress of the bodies. The highly colorized décor of the rooms is muted by the clean, fresh flesh of the subjects.

In a miniature model series of The Belvedere Hotel, Gillette built a scale copy of the famed building and set it on fire to "imagine the pain of losing such an icon."

The fire series, towards the middle of the book, provides the vivid colors of the flame, but still connects with the muted tones of the rest of the images.

Finally, there are the landscapes in "To Wish For," which come at the end of the book.

As the sun comes up, it marks the end of the revelry in the woods and a return to normal life.

Much like a sonnet within a play, Gillette's "To Wish For" is a sojourn of beauty, carnal ecstasy, and requited but perhaps relinquished love, amidst a larger story.

# FOURTH ACT

Part 2 | Act 4     75

# The Carel Dispatch

## LOCAL WRITER BEN DELANEY EMPOWERS EAST END CHARACTERS

**BY BELÉN STRATTON-DELANEY**

Being inspired by your hometown is a blessing and curse: You ultimately are writing what you know, but you are also critical of what you love.

Such is the case with Ben Delaney, who lives a bicontinental life now, with half his year spent in his wife's native Cyprus on a centuries-old beachfront B&B(can we describe writer's bliss any better?), is truly a son of the North Carel area.

His debut novel, "Carel-ing," takes a hard, sobering but never judgmental look at characters Long Islanders have long interacted with but perhaps forgotten.

"You're always going to have North Carel and the economics that come with it, because Long Island will always need people to do the jobs they don't want to do," said Delaney about his characters,

Part 2 | Act 4    77

who often are in menial positions or trying to find a ploy to make some easy money. Such is the case with the pivotal book-ending stories of his luminous short story collection, where the characters try to cash in on a loophole in a mattress return policy.

Part Southern Gothic, part Noel Coward, Delaney deftly toes the line between poverty porn and sentimental boot- strap-lifting. His characters experience some ladder-up moments where they might overcome their circumstances, but it's never an enthusiastic run to climb.

A young FIT student, a once-successful jingle writer, a teacher honored for connecting to troubled youth: all fall victim to the stagnancy that defines the main character of the anthology, the cultivated roles in North Carel that just touches the grand estates of Carel, but never in spirit.

Accomplishing what "Hillbilly Elegy" set out to do and what wunderkind Edouard Louis described in the *New York Times* as "autofiction, something France has been doing for more than 10 years," Delaney is quiet in his sagaciousness, never exploiting his characters to some exhaustive diatribe on why they need to improve or how they can do better.

Never overtly political, "Carel-ing" takes a stark look at humanity and survival interspersed with humor and rarities of compassion, like the injured feral cat that unexpectedly finds a home in one story.

"These stories were 20 years in the making," said Delaney, with the last story written in 2017. Spanning his time as an undergraduate at Long Island University to his graduate program in Indiana, to his current life as a father and an international citizen, Delaney's collection is one to evoke nostalgia for those from the area and a sense of wonder from those who have always poked fun at Northern Carel.

With plenty of motifs — like with the Ozymandias-esque often-desecrated statue of Hiram Stratton, a broken-down building

# In the Light of Men

where a bakery once stood — perhaps a luxury few could envision in a town as destitute, "Carel-ing" reads as casually, delightfully and "Long Island" as a bacon, egg and cheese on a roll with salt/pepper/ketchup.

# FIFTH ACT

Part 2 | Act 5    81

# Law school application essay: Belén Aguilar
(Excerpts)

THERE ARE MANY REASONS WHY PEOPLE SAY they want to go to law school... the answer for me is my dad.

For as long as I could remember, my father went to work at some ungodly hour (3:00 a.m. some months) to return home at 8 p.m.

For years, I saw him put in an entire week's worth of work and overtime just to enjoy a weekend with family activities and televised sporting events.

As a Jets fan, Sunday football was not as therapeutic for my dad as it should have been.

## SAM DESMOND

I think of how my father ploughed through years of more difficult work than I ever will do, sans fanfare.

I know I am not the only person in the world with a father like mine.

In fact, there are a myriad of people in my life who I see perform the same silent heroism every day; many accomplish it with a smile.

In a lot of ways, the middle class is the middle child of the world—forgotten amidst the pleading of the poor and the rantings of the rich.

While it is easy to sell your soul to the wealthy or give your heart to the downtrodden, it takes a special dedication to fight for the rights of those neither privileged nor deserted because of the deeper understanding necessary.

These people do not dream of million-dollar homes or mere shelter but a comfort that never seems to exist, no matter how hard they fight.

Even when toeing every line, dotting every 'i', there never seems to be a moment where an honest lifetime's work pays off.

This is my 'why' for law school. It is not to be wealthy or, to be dramatic, or even to help.

It is to level the playing field for those caught in the societal valley of the middle class, the working class, who sink as the ends go to their extremes."

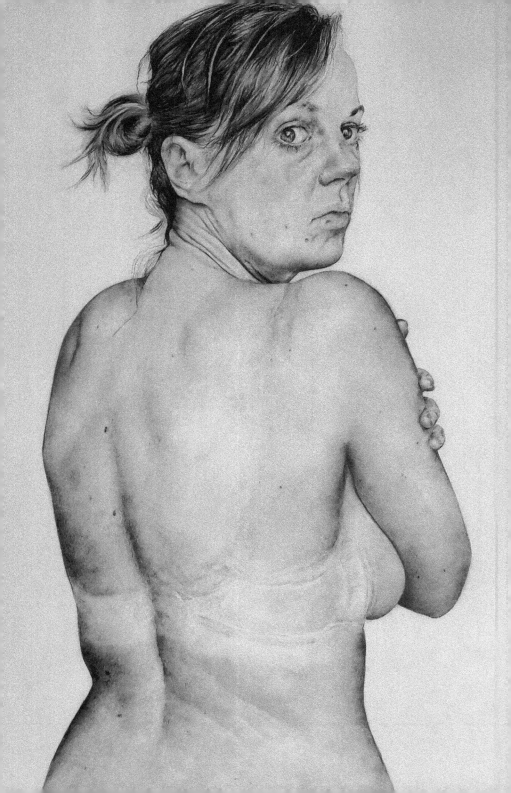

# Part 3

# The Conservatives

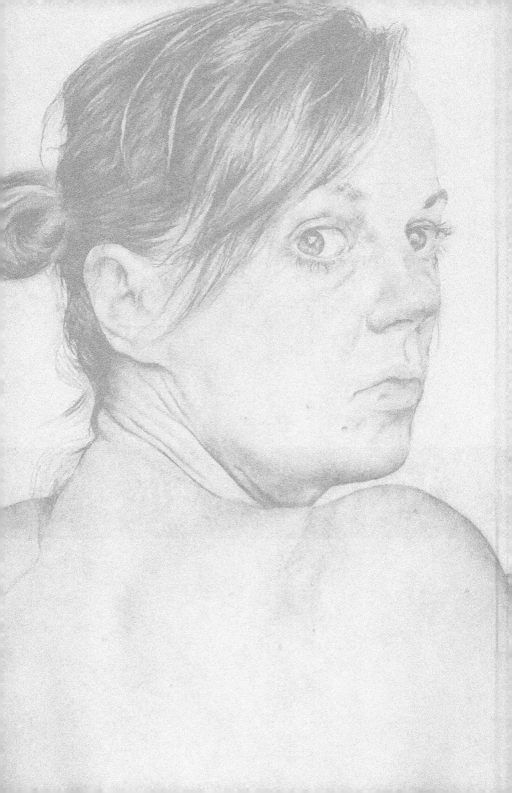

# FIRST ACT

Part 3 | Act I   89

# THE MENTIONABLE PLACE

I've fought the enemy on every front,
    only to strangle myself in victory
For what laurels did I have to grace
    my ravaged mind?
But the numbness of a potent foe

Each day I surrendered to a potion,
    mixed by an alchemist whose
    lust was governed by the
    line below

When I looked outside my windows,
    my soul saw only bars,
    my voice heard only by my
    spiraling consciousness

All tactics in a civil war
    I didn't declare
But one I hoped to survive

I bleed each day from wounds that left no scar

# In the Light of Men

Words are no longer the weaponry
    I once thought I had
This battle has damned my speech
    through my damned thoughts

The enemy twisted my propaganda
    and I fell for my own prophecies
Awakening to a nightmare thought to be shut out,
    but instead went to bed with

Infecting what little honor I had left
There were no battle hymns,
    only ballads for the departed

My hero could not stay by my side
The fires would claim his
    spirit, had he tried

Each march into the dawn
    brought only a realization that
    there was no end,
Only more footsteps to fall

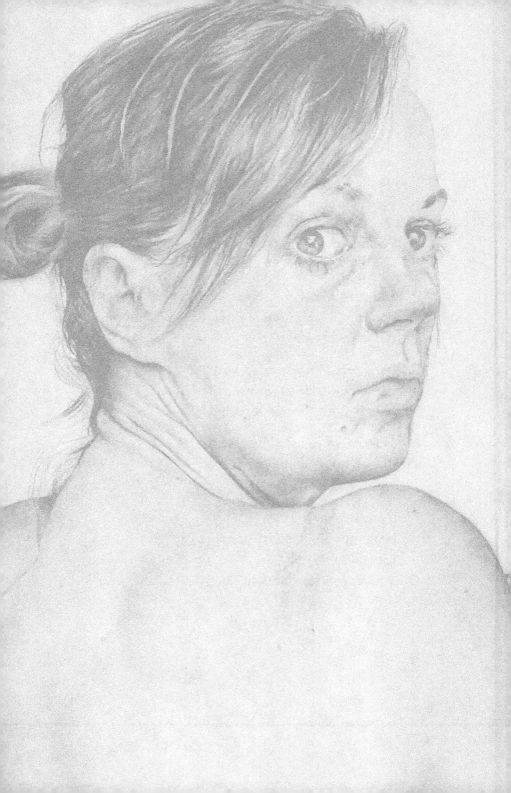

# SECOND ACT

Part 3 | Act 2 95

SHOULD SHE BLAME THE AMBIEN AGAIN THIS time? Would he buy her story that she had no idea what she was texting to him the night before? Maybe it was time to finally give up on him? He made it clear a million subtle times he wasn't interested in her, but she just couldn't let him be polite about it. She had to go overboard with overtures and proposition him head-on. She looked back at her phone and winced at what she wrote and winced even harder at his hours of non-replies.

"It's so hard to have a crush on you."

"Why don't you want me? Is it because of my weight?"

"But we have an open marriage!"

Finally, he answered with, "What is the matter with you? You're married to one of my friends."

And, of course, she couldn't leave it at that. No. She had to call him. At least there was the sweet release of not remembering what he said on the call.

Well, not *precisely* remembering. She remembered he did say, "I'm not into that. I'm not okay with it."

Translation: If you were hotter or just more impressive as a person, I'd have said "yes." I'd have said "yes" a long time ago. She knew he'd fucked at least one other married woman. Was it a worse fate than other women in his past who had been fucked before they were forgotten? No, she couldn't even get there. She'd always be the geek who couldn't get laid, who didn't quite understand the outrage at Brock Turner because she not-so-secretly dreamed of having someone sexually assault her.

Of course, safely, by someone she was attracted to in the first place.

But her husband never made her feel desired. Not as a woman. Not even as a girl. Their first night together, she had to convince him to take her virginity. "No, come on, put your shirt back on." In response, she took off her bra. He told her she was beautiful. That he found her to be the most beautiful girl—*woman*—in the world. But it all felt hollow. Every repetition made it seem even more preposterous. And why always "beautiful"? That was for souls, not bodies.

But with her husband, it was more disappointment than anything else. He was too good for her. Too noble. Too handsome. Too understanding. Too steadfast. It was the reason why she could let him fuck someone else, not that he ever did. But he could. And even with *copious* permission, she *couldn't*. And now it was all in black and white—or pink and green, as she had changed her phone background to—to see. He didn't want her. Even if having an affair was okay. Even if he wasn't entangled with a wife of his own.

She wrote him an apology text that morning. "I'm sorry for the tough and awkward position I put you in yesterday" ('yesterday' sounded less whore-ish than 'night') and "I value your friendship highly." She knew he wouldn't answer her back. She didn't even have his tenuous friendship anymore. Her impatience to hit the sheets had cost her her only grasp of him.

She told her husband what she had sent to him, and he rolled his eyes, knowing her childish and moronic ideas of lust had cock-blocked her yet again. Why did Lifetime make affairs seem so common? Why did society make men seem so willing? Why did she seem so tone-deaf to the mating ritual? Because she lived in fantasy. And she didn't need to.

She had the best husband in the world. One who told her she was beautiful after gaining 150 pounds. One who loved her enough to coach her to lose that weight. One who understood the medication made it more difficult. This all led into why she couldn't be with *just* him. She didn't deserve him. Not at her best and certainly not at her current. He loved her in spite of her flaws and sometimes because of them.

She deleted his contact information from her phone and the hundreds of text messages between them. Part of her was upset that he acted like he didn't see it coming. Like she was a guy who just got "friend-zoned."

Maybe he was saving face. Maybe he was following what he deemed standard protocol. Maybe he was honestly a good man who didn't want to involve himself with a married woman. He told her last night, "I really like you as a friend." The role that ended her treasured world of fantasy. But did it even have anything to do with him? Or did she just want to feel the rush of pursuit? Something she had never experienced from someone she was attracted to. Maybe that's why she had

SAM DESMOND

always wanted married men before. It meant that they had to defy society to want her. It meant she couldn't twist it in her head that they weren't attracted to her. It meant the world to her, and her husband understood this. She didn't deserve him. He deserved a beautiful, dutiful wife who could earn a good living and actually be his partner. His one flaw was loving her. Secretly, she hoped he'd get drunk and disappear for hours like he used to because it would at least give her a tangible flaw to bring up as she tried to seduce other men. But now she was making it worse, painting herself to be a harlot as her husband rolled his eyes at her clumsy attempts.

Her husband had 53—*at least* 53—confirmed women before her. She knew this because, in a jealous tantrum early in their relationship, she went through his phone asking about every female entry. Did you fuck her? How many times did you fuck her? Was she good? What parts of her body do you remember the most? Maybe if having given him her virginity had been more sacred to him instead of odd she wouldn't be having this latent rebellion to fuck more people to prove she could. She wanted someone to wail like Otis did because of her. Other than her husband. But it would never be any guy she wanted.

She kept checking her phone, knowing he'd never text her enough for her to stop wanting to hear from him. Maybe she would've been better off having her heart broken a few times before she got married so she could appreciate what she had instead of taking it for granted out of what was really boredom. But this had been her entire experience with men she was attracted to and unfortunately revealed her feelings to.

In her past, there was the English teacher who spent so much time with her cultivating her talent, reassuring her of her beauty, joking with her like an adult. She tearfully held her yearbook for him to sign and almost as tearfully told him that she wanted him. Of course, he did the right thing and said, "As much fun as this would be for me, I can't. I saw John Mahoney in 'Moonstruck' and vowed I'd never be that teacher."

Of course, being seventeen, she didn't quite give up and took bolder chances, wore skimpier clothes. Bought thigh highs and a garter belt from Victoria's Secret with the credit card her parents regrettably thought she was responsible enough for as a teenager.

One solitary study hall where she sat next to him, she leaned back in her chair, crossed her ankles, lifted her paired, stockinged legs up, and landed her feet softly on his lap. There was a glimmer of a smile on his face, and she thought she'd won, but instead, he backed away and asked—*threatened*—"Do I need to start avoiding you?" Just like he did last night.

That's always when it stopped being fantasy and she would be devastated at the thought of losing the halfway relationship she wished had been more. But what was the point of the conversations, of all the 'understanding,' of all the mentorship if not to fuck at the end of it? Didn't a passionate kiss after a high-five slapping conversation make sense to anyone else? Why was society dead set on convincing her that men were always angling for

SAM DESMOND

sex when it was her embarrassing experience that they didn't want it when she was willing?

It was one of the few points in her marriage that made her feel physically desirable. She had withheld any intellectual or deep conversation with her husband when they first started dating. She was nearly dead silent. Agreeable. Stupid, even. He *had* to have found her physically attractive to have wanted to be with her despite the lack of mental connection. But now she felt that's all they were and whatever beauty he thought she possessed was tied into respect and therefore untrue.

And every woman wanted to be seen as physically attractive. Only "ugly chicks needed feminism." She was sure even Gloria Steinhem stared at her stomach and thighs in the mirror during the first days of "Ms." wondering how she would look in front of the cameras. She wanted to feel desirable. She wanted to feel as desired as she had felt towards all the men who politely said, "no thank you." The most recent one was just hurting the most.

She thought back to all the recycled memes and GIFs he sent her to make her feel better about "haters" when she felt excluded. The two-minute-long voice messages he left her after 9 o'clock and a long day of work for him. All the times she spoke to her husband about his actions and he assured her he was a man acting interested and flirting. But that was all gone now, all over, because he would never speak to her again. And if she tried to speak to him, he'd ignore it or simply say, "Please don't contact me anymore. Thanks."

But what if she could finally be hot? Have a yoga body to die for like the friend of hers she tried to set him up

In the Light of Men

with, and he went crazy for? Dye her hair even blonder? Just be irresistible? Would he want her? Or would that just get her into the worse position of being fucked and forgotten? Was fate doing her a favor by preserving these relationships as platonic?

No.

It was killing her to stare in the mirror every day and know only other straight women would ever look at her as if she were beautiful. In a completely VW Bug type of way.

Was she the most pitiful of sluts to not even be able to fuck? She had a stepfather. A wonderful, dutiful stepfather who took over the payments after her mother had cut out her own biological father. That was her insecurity always: that she was "loved" out of duty and not truly. That was the "daddy issue" with her latest rejection. Was he just being polite and dutiful, not even as a friend, but for his own sake of being a good man, and ultimately wished of not having her as a burden? She had even hated using the term "stepfather" because she wanted more than anything to be "daddy's little girl." Even as a child, she thanked her stepfather for working overtime, for being a 'real dad, not just a father,' for the gift of taking on a burden that wasn't his.

Now, or perhaps always, it was a romantic need for the same. And she kept receiving the same response of, "I love you but in a secondary, stepchild way."

It was true, she deified any man unfortunate enough to be the focus of her affection. She deified them so she would never be good enough to be their little girl. *Great,* she thought, *I'm as trite as having daddy issues.*

Maybe that was why she had started a new obsession

on Pinterest with miniature fairy gardens. Fairies were naïve, romantic prudes, or awkward virgins. Mermaids were the emblem of tried-and-true sluts and whores. Dollhouses were safe, sterile, and controllable. The dolls had no choice but to follow through on her fantasies. They possessed no real life to disappoint her. They couldn't reject her like they politely did in real life. Like he did. Like the "he" *always* did.

His words kept coming back. She squinted her eyes to keep them blurry as she deleted the texts from the previous night to keep herself from re-reading and remembering in sobriety. But it was no use. Why did she have to call him after he sent those texts? Why did she have to torture herself more? Why didn't he 'politely' let her believe in what she wanted from him? "Well, I value you as a friend." It had to be because she wasn't hot enough. That was a much more palatable rejection. Her whole life, her weight had been the missing piece. Her stepfather had tried to warn her, "You seem to only like white guys; they like their women thin." Everything. Every vice came down to that. The bulimia of her adolescence. The coke of her twenties. The psychotropic meds for the rest of her life.

She fantasized about what her life would be like if it weren't for her husband's constant push to health. She'd be single. She'd weigh at least 400 pounds and would escape every night into mac-and-cheese and Audrey Hepburn movies where she would imagine herself as thin.

In her friendship with her latest rejector, he had told her in his younger days, he always "found it hard to find someone really good-looking" and now in his mid-thirties realized, "it seems the better-looking girls are, the shallower they seem to be." Or maybe it didn't matter what her weight was. She was just too unusual looking for his WASPy sensibilities and his blood lust for trophies. Maybe dyeing her hair blonde made her look even more pathetic. More garishly odd. He said, "It's not because of your weight." But that was clearly still in a state of politeness.

Why did Ambien always let her remember a few details? Now, she would never hear from him. She was always worried he was avoiding her, and now, he didn't even have a polite reason to respond to her mewling texts. She dreaded all the events she'd have to go to knowing he'd be cold to her. And nothing stung like the social avoidance of a WASP. She'd have to endure it, pretend it didn't happen, only to ruminate about it for weeks. Months ago, he had asked her to "cool it with the hugging" if she visited him at work.

"You don't like my hugs?"

"No...I like your hugs. Just not when you're supposed to be formal."

Why didn't he just read her short stories where he was an enviable character? Written as everything he wished to see himself as. As she willed herself to see him, and grander even. Or did he actually read it and feel embarrassed? Did an artist ever seduce a muse with their work, or did it always turn out as painful as the delivery of "The Little Mermaid"? Or van Gogh's ear?

Maybe that's how she should have looked at his final rejection—his way of inspiring.

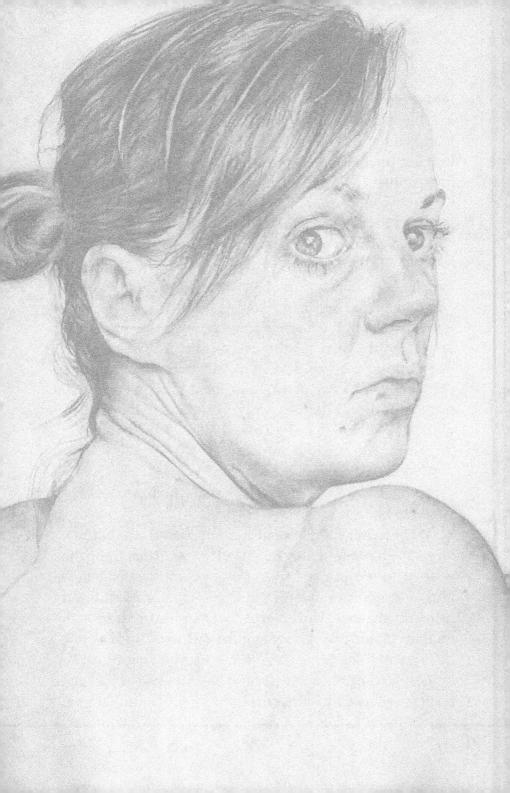

# THIRD ACT

Part 3 | Act 3     107

SHE HAD ALWAYS LOVED WHAT LAY AT THE TOP of society's pyramid.

The royals. The WASPs. The blondes.

She preferred the term "anglophile" but more so lately got "white apologist" or "colonized."

Eschewing bad boys even as a teenager, she always wanted the older man who wielded control from inside a system.

Whether for good or for evil would be based on her whim.

As of late, she had been screenshotting Facebook posts of her most leftist friends to her conservative lover, half-pretending to be incensed, half-agreeing with their ideas.

"Why don't you stick to the teacup girls?" He said to her after sending him a post about ADHD sufferers being "supreme hunter-gatherers" before the cancer of capitalism.

The teacup girls were two special-needs young ladies she had recently written about for the local paper, who made vintage teacup birdfeeders from China they had thrifted or received as donations from a local café and were selling their wares at an organic farm.

Their social worker repeatedly thanked Belén for her help and for choosing to write about them.

## SAM DESMOND

The girls had sold out all 40 bird feeders.

That felt like enough. That felt like a triumph for helping the marginalized. That felt like a good deed.

But it was never enough, and she tossed in her head how "ableist" it probably was for her to focus on "inspiration porn" and write about the young ladies.

That they were from a middle-class, white background probably also didn't help because she wasn't helping the *most* marginalized special-needs people.

It was all too much for her.

Her lover assured her that she was helping the people who "deserved to be helped."

In her own eugenic reflection, she had thought that being unable to work during her bouts of bipolar depression made her someone who couldn't contribute to society and thus, should be removed from it. These young ladies were still trying to make a living and contribute to society, so they should have the benefits to live in it.

She just didn't understand why people felt so entitled, a word they often threw at straight, white men, to admonish and essentially yell at people to accommodate their issues.

Perhaps she just wasn't progressive enough to demand that people respect hers.

There was always a void in her feelings of self-worth because she never thought she had the work ethic, or the steadfastness of her husband, or her father, more straight, white males, who would work for dozens of days without a day off.

Was it really just the horrible endgame of capitalism? Or did people just believe working long hours was the

## In the Light of Men

fault of capitalism and the Protestant work ethic because they couldn't do it themselves, and their self-preservation required them to blame some societal ill to explain it away?

She felt caught between two worlds: one that sought to break apart all the standards and be more equitable and one that sought to adapt itself to be more inclusive.

Both seemed to require more effort than she was willing to give.

Was she really just in love with her captors? A victim of the colonial mentality? A Filipina colorist?

Probably.

But she was so much more at ease in that colonizer world. Just acclamations for her talent, her beauty, her kindness. Never asked for more and always grateful for what she could muster.

Being a revolutionary just seemed like making excuses and tying everything back to some sin of patriarchy, misogyny, white supremacy, capitalism, or homophobia.

In therapy, she learned that "if it's too complicated, it's not true." But then again, her therapist was a beautiful, thin, white woman who taught yoga.

But she felt the most at ease with her. She felt like she made progress in life with her. Or did it just bring her closer to the whiteness that was to blame for so many of the miseries she was told she had in her life?

All the men in her life were conservative, even her self-proclaimed "socialist" husband, who touted union rights for all but still would only live in the southern part of the town he grew up in.

All the white men, anyway.

Part i | Act i   111

SAM DESMOND

Then it struck her that she really *only had* white men in her life.

Her women friends were all white women. Even the trans ones.

It was only normal to feel you should defend your friends, and she did see them as attacked online when a conversation would shut down completely or a "boundary" would be put up simply because they were white.

She always said she wanted racism and sexism to end, that she didn't need her turn as master.

But did serving as master's human pet fit her well enough?

Maybe that's all she was and that was the "white protection" she was told she had.

But the compliments and reassurances of handsome, successful white men made her deliriously happy. It meant *something*. It meant that you had passed the hardest, most demanding test. It meant that you could have whatever you wanted.

And she wasn't even thin and white-looking, so how could all these handsome, successful white men like her *and* be racist with those attributes missing?

Maybe her compliance was enough to make up for it?

God, she was a Candace Owens or a Michelle Malkin.

She shuddered at the thought but then remembered how much more attractive they were than most liberal women. Maybe not AOC.

She thought of her work as a reporter. She thought it probably was all fluff. All testaments to "white privilege," a term she was actually neutral to the first time she read it

In the Light of Men

because she was in a class group with Latinas and was surprised to see how angry the white students were when they came back into the room after the separate group exercise.

Clambakes. Community fairs. Lemonade stands. Feisty pets. She never challenged the system, but even more so, she celebrated it.

In undergrad, during a lesson on Virgil, her professor brought up Aeneas' resistance to marrying Lavinia and said it might be an indication that he was "more than just a cheerleader for the empire."

Maybe that's what she was, a slightly rebellious teenager who wrote positively about the trans teacher at the elementary school as a progressive article she "earned" to give to her audience after writing about 9/11 and military heroes in the town.

And in the white world of liberals, that was enough. That made her a progressive. That made her an ally.

But when the trans teacher got fired for inappropriate social media content (she took an ass shot in her underwear), she didn't write an article vilifying the transphobes who monitored her social media looking for a reason to attack.

In part because she agreed with the school's decision that she went against policy, but also, she decided a big, public fight would make it worse for the teacher.

But was that her right to do so? Or should she have written the article and fought?

Her sojourns into gay people in the community were always of exceptional people, who "earned their right" to be in an upper-middle-class suburb.

Perhaps that was just more imperial and colonizer

Part i | Act i    113

## SAM DESMOND

thoughts in her mind, that marginalized people had to be better to be accepted by the majority.

Her articles about the local government were even more subdued. She usually had her colleague write anything remotely critical about the local government, partly because she didn't want her taxes to go up, partly because she never felt secure enough to criticize any government as a naturalized citizen. There was always a part of her that thought she needed to be the good patriot to keep her place.

Like her favorite painter, David, ingratiating himself with royalty, rebels, and regimental Napoleon. Maybe her loyalty was just to whoever was in power, and that's what caused the turmoil in her thoughts because the criticisms of "centering whiteness" seemed to be in power in the art and literary world, and she didn't know which master to serve.

For her, It was probably easier to be an artist than a reporter, but she always felt like a hybrid of the two. Pulling people in with her eloquence and then hiding broccoli in the mac and cheese by writing about the drag queen shows in the local cat café.

Maybe she actually understood what real oppression felt like being from a third-world country and an immigrant and not being able to speak out against your captors that the little crumbs of progress she could make, the soft sanding of prejudices, was enough progress for her.

But, it was probably, or at least she would be told, borne out of her own privilege.

Her father was blue-collar, union, and someone who definitely did not analyze or acknowledge any privilege he had. He was steadfast that all his possessions came to him

# In the Light of Men

by way of hard, unforgiving work, and she felt this because she understood the privilege *she* gained from having a stable home, food, and resources and a housewife for a mom.

Even her writing ability seemed like a skill she gained from a blue-collar perspective, spending Sunday mornings reading the paper with her father and learning how to write to the "common man" like him.

But if anything, that's where her ambition grew. She fell in love with Jackie O. and created an alter ego named Daphne Lavinia Gwyneth Claire Grosvenor, who was born a "winner" and dated beaux from Eton.

She wanted to honor, but overcome, her blue-collar upbringing and didn't think to be angry when teachers said, "You don't think like the daughter of a bus driver!"

It was like Balenciaga, who grew up with a seamstress for a mother; he could ball up her lessons on how to sew and then transform himself into something accepted by people higher up.

That's how she felt writing for the town she lived in. Her husband's WASP town.

People admired her skill and intelligence, or at least the appearance of it—she wasn't convinced she actually had either—and adored her articles celebrating the milestones of their life and community.

But she felt she truly belonged in the other community, the marginalized one, or now, to be in vogue, "the historically underrepresented" one, the one that she grappled with because her individual experiences didn't line up, but all her demographic factors did.

Could she ever serve both? And did she even want to?

Part I | Act I    115

# Part 4

# The Foreigners

# FIRST ACT

Part 4 | Act 1    119

# GARDEN CONSENT

Intertwined or apart
There is no difference as time passes
Forgetfulness is not the venom in the serpent

Can the ties that bind survive?
Can the light above alone
pull apart the ivy from the stone?

No.

The fight for stolen glances
  covered embraces
  the wonder of your worth

The weed has never been a nurturer
But how can they destroy the structures built forcefully?
Or ruin the bonds that grow naturally?

The sky and gardener decide,
  not the flowers and the weeds

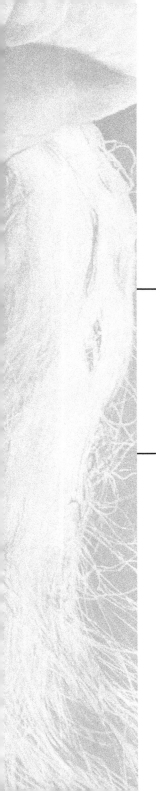

# SECOND ACT

MAYBE SHE WAS ACTUALLY SPECIAL ENOUGH TO get to have two soulmates. She wanted *both* her husband and Cristobal forever. And not as competing entities but as two halves both needed to make her whole. They were similar enough where it mattered, where her dad had also told her it mattered—die-hard work ethic. Whereas her husband was the young groom, Cris was the perennial bachelor nearly in his 50s. But he was responsibly Peter Pan-ish, with no ex-wives and no children. She truly believed he used condoms every time he had sex. After losing his virginity caused a pregnancy scare, he said he never wanted to have that fear ever again. Before she got her tubes tied, she told him about a fantasy where he said "fuck it" to the condom because she felt so good. Assured him she was a liberal and that she'd get an abortion. He said, "I'm pro-choice, but I would feel awful about an abortion because of carelessness."

Whereas her husband always pushed her to strive for never-ending personal 'better' (a therapist that was promptly dropped after making the observation told her she gravitated towards her husband because he was like her Tiger Mom) in her weight, in her job, in her civic-mindedness, Cris let her exist as she was.

SAM DESMOND

When he left for his native Chile for the summer, she said, "Well, at least I'll have two months to get in shape for you," and he replied, "You look super sexy the way you are." He reminded her of the teacher she loved in high school who turned her down when she asked him to take her virginity. They both made her feel beautiful and smart. He let her feel as beautiful and smart *as she was*. Not as a memory or potential.

Her financial fights with Patrick had gotten worse since it had been nearly six years since she got fired from the law firm. Patrick blamed her for all their financial problems. And he was in the right, but she hated how he never appreciated the gravity of her efforts. She had briefly held down two jobs in the last six years, both of meager pay and socially devastating, only to break down and be sick again.

She resented her husband for forgetting that while she had been sick for the past six years, his two car accidents had totaled up to nearly three years of her as the sole breadwinner. But that didn't matter, she could never hold down a job anyway, even before she got sick. She was lazy and selfish. Cris was the one to build up her confidence during the hell of the last month trying to get a job. Patrick said, "You're so lazy you won't even get a job flipping burgers to save our house!" Cris told her, "It's no one's business what you do for a living. And Target is a serious company," when she cried at the idea of being hired to be a cashier in her 30s.

But she landed the better job. The one that would be six figures in a few years' time. Cris said he was proud

## In the Light of Men

of her. Over and over again. She figured that was the reasoning behind the teacher fetish she had—someone in a position of authority whose opinions mattered more because of that, but also had the ability to play second parent where the ones at home fell short. Patrick was her Tiger mom, Cris was her teacher. She needed them both to thrive.

Was she starting to rely on Cris too much? Probably, but he made her feel good, and she hadn't for years. From the first unexpected message that made her feel desirable again to the daily attention to answer her promptly between his classes to the overall beautiful soul he was. She still loved her husband. She was still *in* love with him but felt like he couldn't love her in her current state. He was still in love with a shadow of whom she used to be or a vague silhouette of who she could be. Either way, her husband couldn't love her as she was, but Cris could. Or maybe because he didn't love her, he could accept her as she was.

For the two months he was away, she gleefully obsessed over a list she made of toiletries to leave at his apartment in the city. It would symbolize being a constant, albeit infrequent, element of his life. She fantasized about the day she'd ask him to leave a bag in his fully completed-by-bachelorhood walk-in closet. And he said "yes" when she asked to leave the medium-sized, millennial, Vera Bradley red vanity bag there. Even nonchalantly so, which made her happier.

And she wanted happiness for Cris. Assuming it selfishly didn't put her out of the picture, she wanted

## SAM DESMOND

him to date and meet other women who were hotter and younger because it would mean he still liked her despite the prettier stock available to him. She wanted the same for her husband. Someone young and beautiful and in great shape. Someone like she used to be, but better. Someone who could hold down a good job. Someone who wasn't clinically crazy. Someone who could have children. During their last fight, Patrick said, "That's why I would never have kids with *you*!" He said it was purposely meant to hurt but never rescinded the message. She was always sorry he fell in love with her instead of a pretty, normal, bubbly elementary school teacher who would have been an equal financial partner with her New York, union salary and given him a perfect, easy life with a clean house and children, having only gained 25 pounds with each pregnancy that she would lose easily. The current girl Patrick was seeing was all of that with a second job in tow.

But Cris didn't need, or even want her to be that. Perhaps because he didn't want her as a wife, and it was fine to be a loser as a friend. But he only seemed to see her bright side, even as she fell apart in every text she sent. He always reminded her of what good she was and could be. Her high school teacher, after her tubal ligation, had said, "It's better for the world that now you don't have to focus on something as mundane as childbirth; your brilliant mind deserves much more."

She looked at her phone. Her husband's and her lover's (as her best friend told her to refer to him) phone numbers stacked on top of each other for her most recent

## In the Light of Men

texts. She wrote, "I love you so much. I miss you" to one and "I love you. Can't wait to see you" to the other.

# THIRD
# ACT

Part 4 | Act 3    131

# The Carel Dispatch

## PIONEERS' OF 300-YEAR-OLD BRITISH SCHOOL TO BECOME PART OF CAREL

**BY BELEN STRATTON DELANEY**

With a storied tradition of opulence and the requisite noblesse oblige, Carel, a community famous for its sprawling historical mansions, connections to the robber barons of the Gilded Age, and currently boasting a robust community civic spirit, is the perfect setting for Crofton School to open its much-anticipated New York outpost.

Major renovations to the main structures and 170 acres are taking place at Archibald Mansion with local construction giant, Kerrigan Construction and grounds renewal by Carel Horticulture.

The opening of Crofton New York, the first Crofton International School in the United States, is slated for next autumn.

# In the Light of Men

The original Crofton School, located in the United Kingdom, was founded by Earl William Crofton by royal charter of King George 1 over 300 years ago and has since produced five Prime Ministers, including Philippa Raspell.

As a side note, Carel's founding father descendant Eudora Stratton was rumored to have borne a child out of wedlock fathered by Raspell's brother, Edith, who was adopted and eventually became a U.S. Senator.

Sartorially, Crofton students have been distinguished with a more light-hearted and whimsical uniform consisting of elegant capes and Rembrandt-esque hats that can only be purchased from centuries-old milliner shop, Guildstetter's in London.

"We are setting out to restore the mansion and grounds to its former glory," said Cristobal Santana, who will be serving as Headmaster of Crofton New York, an alumnus of the original UK school graduating in 1988.

Santana, a native of Chile, after graduating from Crofton School and Cambridge University, went on to have a successful career as the lead singer of Nomini Patri in the early- to mid-nineties touring Latin America, Asia, and Europe before becoming a music teacher at Crofton UK following the tragic death of the band's guitarist and drummer in an apparent intentional overdose of heroin.

With waterfront property, the Georgian-style mansion built in 1897 for Nathaniel Archibald, the president of Mercury Typewriters, will house approximately 80 students per graduating year from grades 6 through 9, subsequently adding a grade each year thereafter.

The school is currently awaiting its Provisional Charter from the New York State Education Department and expects this to be approved soon. In addition, Crofton New York has been accepted as a Candidate School to offer the International Baccalaureate Diploma Programme in grades 11 and 12.

# SAM DESMOND

A co-educational (Crofton UK is strictly split with a boys section and girls section) school with both boarding and day students, along with the option for weekly boarding (i.e., living on campus Monday through Friday with home visits Saturday and Sunday), Crofton New York is said to "offer a bespoke and challenging academic curriculum, combined with pastoral care of the highest standard and an outstanding co-curricular program, all rooted firmly in the Crofton values of Honor, Service, and Humility," according to the school's website.

"I've had top-tier faculty from around the world contact me," said Santana, "Crofton opening a school in New York is the biggest news right now in the international education community."

While Santana highlighted the unique opportunities for learning available in New York City, only 60 miles away, he is adamant that the Crofton tradition and spirit cannot thrive without a strong relationship with the local community.

"We're not here to hide behind big gates," said Santana, "We want our students and faculty to make connections with local civic groups and community members to investigate opportunities where they can make a difference."

Among the community integration ideas is the potential use of the campus by the Carel Civic Association and Carel Heritage Association for their monthly meetings and for special celebrations such as Earth Day.

The popular 5K charity event held on July 4 and previously organized by Carel Civic Association president, Michael Kim is another community event that Santana is keen to revive.

"We as a community are excited for the opening of Crofton International. We are looking forward to the school bringing new life to the grounds of the Archibald Mansion as well as the Carel community. The Carel Civic Association looks forward to working together with Crofton and possibly returning the successful Carel

## In the Light of Men

Firecracker 5K to the grounds in the future. We are also looking forward to the possibility of Crofton allowing the civic to use their grounds going forward to host our monthly civic meetings. I anticipate the opening of the school bringing nothing but positives to our community," said Kim.

Myrtle Baylor Almstead, president of the Carel Heritage Association, who met with Crofton officials earlier in the year said she was "pleasantly surprised" at the organization's celebration and intent to preserve and restore the history of the property.

"And we really, really like the hats!" said Baylor Almstead.

# FOURTH ACT

Part 4 | Act 4

# WORDSMITHS

Writers barter for favorable opinions
    in order to be authors
Give a glimpse of your work
    mitigating would-be competitors

All too sensitive for true criticism

All reading to condemn…
    Trite!
    Banal!
    Plagiarized!

We all learn grander words to say this

Who is most attuned to emotion?
    most observant of nature?
    most perverted in delivery?

Posthumous popularity—
    rarely is it given without
gutting a corpse

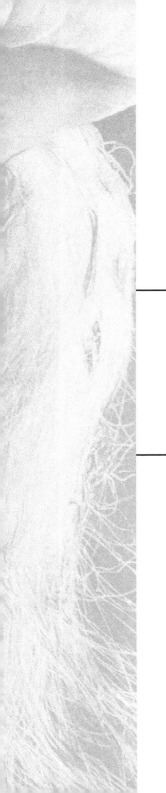

# FIFTH ACT

GRANT HAD SAID, "WE GET DIFFERENT THINGS from different people," and she certainly felt fulfilled differently by Patrick and Cristobal. The cool breeze off the bay and the playfully bright sun on the ferry ride over to Cherry Grove made the young, beautiful men on board gleeful with flirtations.

*How lovely to be young and gay,* she thought. In a past life, she must've been a gay man, it only made sense why they understood her so well. And there was always an element of sluttiness to her, even if the actual number of people she slept with didn't reflect the harlot spirit within.

As the ferry docked, she saw Grant standing, that proud back of his with his chin turned slightly upward. A true Southern gentleman with his staple Ray Ban clubmasters to hide his judgment. She thought he'd wear linen as a Southerner, but he didn't.

She went to the lower level of the ferry to disembark. There was an overwhelming smell of coke amongst the crowd. Patrick had told her years ago, when she first started to do coke, that it had a gasoline smell to it, and she picked up on it now. How she missed how thin she was during the heyday of her coke usage. The ADHD

SAM DESMOND

meds were no comparison, but with age came the need for a more reliable drug dealer.

She ran over to Grant, who offered her a big hug.

"How are you, sweetie?" he said in his Southern drawl, tamed by years of being a New Yorker.

"Ehhh, always good, but never at peace."

"Isn't that the way?"

"I don't want it to be the way. We're spending $350 a week on therapy to get it to stop being that way."

"I know. But at least you're working through it."

They passed by a group of young, beautiful men, twinks, and unicorns as Grant would call them.

"You must be having a blast surrounded by all these adventures," she said coyly.

"Oh no. I come out here to write. I don't even go to the beach."

"I admire how you're a 'cabin-in-the-woods' writer, I can't do it unless I'm happy and in the mood."

"That's youth, but I know you also don't write about anything unless it's truly important. You are fabulous at it, though."

She loved getting compliments from Grant about her writing. He was the first person she ever sent a new piece to because she admired him so much as a writer.

"The food is much better here than the Pines. But I'm staying there with Geoff Covalent and his husband. I have a makeshift bed in the laundry room."

"No! Don't tell me that, I want to hear how gay and fabulous and rich everyone is. You're gay royalty."

"Am I? I don't feel that way."

## In the Light of Men

"Well, you're certainly snobby enough."

"I am not a snob."

"What about Juan's boyfriend?"

"What about him?"

"You constantly made fun of him being dumb because he didn't know politics."

"Well, he knew hair…"

"See?"

"Oh, he wasn't going to make Juan happy! He was from Staten Island for goodness sake!"

"Well, as a Queens girl, I have to agree with that sentiment."

They sat down at an oceanside restaurant. The table was indoors, but with large, open windows that let in the breeze.

The waitress, a local girl from the mainland town, probably a lacrosse star in the fall, came by with menus and a big smile.

"What imported beers do you have?" Grant asked seriously.

"Well, we have Corona—"

Deadpan, Grant remarked, "No, honey, this is supposed to be a GAY bar…"

He pondered a moment, "I'll have a mojito," Grant said, relieved, "Now I have an excuse to hit the liquor earlier in the day."

"I'll have an unsweetened iced tea," Belén said.

"Oh, 'cause of the meds?"

"Yeah, it's not much fun with them anyway."

"Well, good for you, you're really trying. Patrick must be happy. He adores you."

# SAM DESMOND

"I know. He's the reason I'm trying to get better."

"Yes, I know how much you two love each other."

"I just wish he were more understanding of what I needed from him right now. I know he says and thinks he means that 'I want you to be healthy' means just that, but all I hear is 'I want you to be thin like you used to be.'"

"He doesn't really seem like someone who says what he doesn't mean."

"That's what I love about Cris. He always says I don't need to lose weight, and I guess because he's Latino, I can believe he likes bigger women?"

"What do I always say? Different things from different people. Ted and I are married, but we get fulfillment from other people. Maybe it's different for straight people. Maybe heteros don't ever really understand what an 'open marriage' really is."

"I guess. I just wish I could combine them."

"See? There's your problem, you're not letting people be people, you have to take the whole person. It's like a character, they can't all be everything or there's no story."

She sighed and stared at her phone.

"Oh God, you're not still sending those desperate texts to Cris about getting him to tell you you're pretty, are you?"

She stared at Grant with a look between shame and exasperation.

"Sweetie, nothing makes a dick more flaccid than insecurity," he took a sip of his drink, "Maybe using too many emojis."

In the Light of Men

"Oh, like that young guy you started talking to?"

"Yeah, I can't do that. He was literally texting me every 5 minutes. With nothing. NOTHING. Just a string of emojis, like desperate hieroglyphics."

"Still dreaming of Brandon?"

"Always, and I always will pine for him."

"Did you get that gig for him as the guest writer at The New Yorker?"

"…Maybe…"

"You're like his fairy godfather." She thought about the statement she made and added, "that wasn't a homophobic categorization."

Grant pursed his lips and rolled his eyes. "Sweetie, fairy is kind, and godfather makes me feel like a daddy, so we're good."

"Is that what it is about Brandon, why you continue to get him opportunities even though he hasn't shown you any romantic interest? You get to feel like Daddy to him?"

Grant pondered for a second. "I suppose. I hug my pillow at night and pretend it's him."

"That is so beautifully tragic."

"I'm good, I know."

"What is it about Brandon? I know he's good-looking, but you are just so stuck on him."

"He's masculine and feminine at the same time. He's so broken. He's so ambitious. He's so wanting of more renown. And that just drives me to help him."

"But you never feel taken advantage of?"

"I feel honored to be asked."

Part 4  |  Act 5     147

## SAM DESMOND

"Do you think there's something wrong with me that I can't be in the 'giving' position?"

"Oh my God, if this is you trying to figure out if you're a top or a bottom—"

"No, no. I just feel like I constantly need men, more men, to take care of my insecurities, and even when they do, I'm not happy."

"Well, that's what an insecurity is. It has to do with you, not them. My insecurity is getting older without someone to take care of me. Ted is twenty years older than I am. He's going to die, and then I won't have someone."

"So you're hoping Brandon will take care of you?"

"Maybe. Or maybe I'm just a glutton for punishment, and unrequited love makes me write. Who knows?"

"They both make me want to write."

"See? That's all you need."

"It just doesn't feel right to love both of them."

"What level of privilege is this we're discussing now?"

"I know, I just feel like I have to choose between them at some point."

"That's convention talking. You do what you want."

"Part of me wants Cris to ask me to leave Patrick."

"Do you want to leave Patrick?"

"No, I just want Cris to ask."

"That kinda makes you a cunt."

She laughed, "I know. It works. Patrick is my primary, and since Cris needs lots of solitude, he's fine with only seeing me once a month or so."

"And he puts up with all your texts."

"Yes," she sat back, "I am just being greedy, aren't I?"

*In the Light of Men*

"Yes, but you also love them both. And they both love you."

"But you can love Brandon without getting love back?"

"He does give me love back. A love that works for me. And that's what's important."

She sat back and looked out at the ocean.

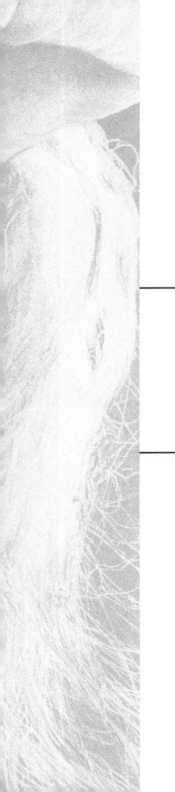

# SIXTH ACT

# THE SMALLEST METROPOLIS

If I receive cruelty, I want it from a memorable face,
I'm hurt more by the nameless masks and a false voice.

We'll move to the world's smallest metropolis
Where everyone's mask turns,
  and falls off at night
Where we see faces, but not the identical features
Where we feel the air from water

We'll pay the price
We can change ourselves to fill the space
  allowed
They know best
This is what we want
This will complete us once we shed
  what we cannot take
I will never want for sorrow to write
For I will have the dawn to dream

# SEVENTH ACT

Part 4 | Act 7   155

Belén texted Blair.

I asked Cris why he couldn't even address that I asked him to come with me to the restaurant and musical I was reviewing in a timely fashion, and he gave me this whole spiel that Saturday night is his only 'me' time and thought I'd feel better by telling me that last Saturday he dicked out of going to a show by the filler-faced teenager he used to teach.

Oh God, men are all fucking the same.

I know. I even said, 'Well I'm glad the jailbait hottie couldn't get you to go out either.

Get other dick. He'll be back around.

## SAM DESMOND

> I need to focus on getting myself to look the way I want to and get better dick.

You look fucking great.

> Yeah, but I'm 40 and fat. Not 18 and skinny. And dick will always pick the latter.

I can't believe he's dating a student.

> Well, I haven't established dating, but you know musicians and teachers are the worst about wanting to fuck teenage girls. And he's both of those things. She actually just turned 18.

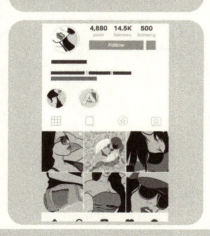

Part 4 | Act 7

SAM DESMOND

> She's extremely fucking basic—wait, are the baby brunette photos of her too?!

Yup, she's a plastic surgery influencer special. She got invited to the Glossier opening in SoHo, so another reason to be jealous.

> And she's a fucking songwriter who idolizes Taylor Swift... you know my love for John Mayer!

I just hate this. No matter how below par a man is, he can always make a woman feel like shit because he falls for some hot, young thing.

> You're successful and hot and established. She's gonna end up with an eating disorder and a drug problem after being denied in the music world and aging out.

Aa

Part 4 | Act 7

## In the Light of Men

> She did just play on Z100.

> Eh fuck her, you've got better dick.

> I'm texting him this---
> I'm just hurt that you'd rather put your time and effort into jailbait that probably thinks of you like her dad's creepy friends. But I guess you can't help who or what you want, and I'll just have to find someone else to distract myself with because you can't even manage to appreciate memes from me.

She blocked his number and un-followed him on Instagram.

Aa

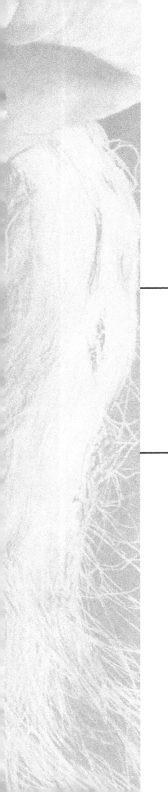

# FINAL ACT

Part 4 | Final Act

I don't know if you saw this one—it was a while back, but important to me that you read it:

I thought about it more today— and I owe you another apology.

I know, and you've made it clear, how important, valued, and necessary alone time is for you to be well, and I shouldn't have asked to come over knowing you had such little time between being with your family 24/7 for all of summer break and having to go straight into school.

I'm sorry I put my wants before your needs.

I love you very much, and I always want to be someone in your life who brings you joy and not burden.

Love you too, dear.

Aa

# Part 5

# The Union Man

# FIRST ACT

Part 5 | Act I    169

PRINCESS DIANA'S TRAGIC AND UNEXPECTED death in 1997 created two lifelong benchmarks of perfection for Belén Aguilar—the British and blondes. That evening, Belén was being babysat by her parents' friends, Morty and Gina, both in their thirties with a new house and baby dutifully minding their neighbor's preteen daughter as her parents attended a wedding. It was late, "Saturday Night Live" was on, and when the NBC special report came on telling the horrific news of the Parisian tunnel demise, Belén did not know what to think of her favorite show's unamusing skit about the death of one of her mother's idols. When she changed the channel and found the news of the car crash everywhere else, she felt ashamed that she had managed a sarcastic guffaw before when she thought it was a joke.

The news story then started to focus on Diana's young children. As the eldest sister to a three-year-old and a newborn, Belén had waited to see rosy-cheeked cherubs be brought forward with little understanding of what had happened. Instead, the news station began to show footage of a tall, exceedingly handsome blond boy in a button-down blue shirt and khakis. Belén had already started to become understandably "boy-crazy"

SAM DESMOND

at eleven (much to the embarrassed horror of her militantly Catholic, Filipina-immigrant mother), but this new object of affection would re-colonize her mind for the rest of her life. The sun glistened off his crown of golden hair. The sky competed with his deep-blue eyes. The gold standard, Belén would come to name this exhibition of recessive genetic traits.

A couple of days after Belén saw her prince, she found an old *People* magazine whose cover Prince William had graced. He wore a white button-down shirt and black pants as he rowed and gave a smoldering look. Inside the magazine, there were photographs of him playing rugby and sporting the Etonian tails. On top of her Aryan preference, Belén was soon becoming an anglophile. Baz Luhrman's "Romeo and Juliet" came out the same year, and she fell in love with the Bard through the brooding blond who played the star-crossed lover. She would watch the movie over and over again whilst reading along with a copy of Folger's *Romeo and Juliet*. Amidst the explosion of pre-pubescent fascination, she started to develop a real affinity for Elizabethan drama.

The cruel joke of fate was that she was destined to grow up in New York in two of the strongest bastions of guido culture that diametrically opposed her fair-haired, knight-in-shining-armor fetish/fantasy. Where would Belén find someone tall, blond, dashing, and chivalrous amongst the Joeys, Tommys, Tonys, and Mikeys that pervaded her hometowns in Queens and Long Island? She longed to live with WASPs and could not be farther from them.

Belén spent the majority of high school aloof and

172     Part 5 | Act ɪ

## In the Light of Men

rebellious through fashion choices. She wore pea coats from army/navy stores before they were popular. She decorated her entire room with visions of England, including a life-sized poster of a London telephone booth. She had resigned herself into believing she would spend high school alone, especially as she cut classes to take trips to Museum Mile and learned that on the Upper East Side, blonds were not as far as she had imagined. When she graduated her senior year, she was ready to pounce and lamented that her parents would not permit her to go to St. Andrews, where William was matriculated.

Her first semester in college in Manhattan, Belén found him.

While standing at the top of the stairs on Track 18 in Penn Station waiting for the Long Island Rail Road's 3:14 to Ronkonkoma, she spotted a tow-headed boy with the close-set, piercing grey eyes of a hunter. She walked down the stairs slowly, waiting for him to make some sort of misstep, but he didn't. Instead, he made a genuine smile at one of his friends, and Belén wished the gracious, warming smile was for her. As many of her crushes went, she doubted this one would ever be requited because, despite her undying allegiance to the gold standard, she was a pathetic inverse bearing dark hair and dark skin.

A couple of days passed and Belén saw him standing at the same spot on the platform with the same group of men. By this time, she had been fantasizing about being enveloped in his lovely set of arms—protective and strong but not vulgar in form like the meatheads that

Part 5 | Act i    173

characterized her pitiful hometown. It was a Thursday, and Belén galvanized herself to take a chance. When she got up to disembark at her stop, she turned around holding her books close to her chest and stared at her yellow-haired, would-be Lothario. She caught his gaze, and he did not move away; she smiled sheepishly. For the next few minutes, she would catch his eyes for a moment and then quickly dart away. Leaping off the train, Belén was proud of herself that she had taken a stance and made an effort, knowing it would likely progress no further.

But this was not to be the case. The next day, as Belén shuffled to find a seat, she passed by his row. It was a three-seater, and he sat alone. She was well past him but was taken over by some energy to go back. After rudely pushing past the people behind her, but politely apologizing, she took a seat in the row he was in, leaving the middle seat open as a buffer. Her entire body had turned red—not that it would be obvious with how dark she was. She was sweating profusely and looking straight ahead, not willing to risk a sideways glance of rejection. A few seconds passed by and a beer can came into her field of vision. It was the largest beer can she had ever seen. Then she heard a voice, more surfer than the nasal Long Island accent.

"Hey, can I offer you a drink?" Even that close his hair still shone brightly and now she could really see how pensive his blue-grey eyes were.

"Sure, I'd love one." She didn't want one. She had to drive home from the train station and didn't even really know what beer tasted like.

"So, are you in college?"

"Ummm…yeah."

"What are you studying?"

"In—International Marketing." Belén looked down again; she wondered what was happening to her as normally she never managed to stop talking.

"My name is Patrick." He extended his hand out, and Belén shook it timidly.

"My name is Claire." Belén's mind stopped and began questioning itself as to why she just lied. Claire had been the name of her favorite actress at the time, and she loved how WASPy of a name it was.

"So where do you live, Claire?"

"In the city, on Park and 68th." *What the hell am I doing? This is awful.* Belén thought as she realized she was ruining her one and only chance with someone who had fit her needs and, more importantly, lived up to her wants.

"You're a ways from home. What brings you out here?"

"I'm visiting my roommate; she lives in Deer Park and I've been helping her with her sick grandmother." The lies were just spouting off terribly, but she was a woman possessed. How could she tell him the truth of where she was actually from and ruin the image she wanted him to have of her?

"So, did you grow up in the city your whole life?"

"Yes, born and raised."

"Long Island must be terribly boring for you. I mean, with everything you have in the city." *Yes, it was boring, wretched, deprived of culture,* Belén thought.

## SAM DESMOND

"It's not too bad. I think the town where my roommate is from is rather gauche..."

"No disagreement here. I mean, Deer Park is in the middle of the island, you go that far from the water on an island, you're asking for some pretty stupid people."

"Is that what it is? The lack of water? Funny, there's a water company called Deer Park water."

Patrick laughed, a genuine laugh, and then he smiled at her, and she melted. Here was someone who fit her description of perfection. He was seeing her as she wanted to be seen.

"Now my town, Carel, is right on the water. It's the most beautiful place on Earth. I would never leave. My family doesn't anyway. My mother's family has been there since the early 1700s, the Strattons. And my dad's family, the Delaneys, have been there since the 1800s."

Belén was somewhat disappointed at his allegiance to Long Island and lack of desired mobility, but his earnest love of his hometown intrigued her.

"I've never been to Carel."

"Of course not, a city girl like you? But you pass by it on your way to the Hamptons. Carel was the original Hamptons. We had Revolutionary War soldiers in our town, and three came from my family. And the Civil War, too, from both sides."

"Really?"

"Yeah, totally. You should come by. Maybe I can show you around sometime..." Patrick's voice wavered at the end of the sentence. Belén's insecurities went into overdrive; she wondered if he meant his offer or if he

176    Part 5  |  Act i

# In the Light of Men

was just being courteous and making polite conversation. She read in *The Preppy Handbook* that WASPs were notorious for that. She sat in silence, no clue what to say next. Patrick was starting to appear perplexed as well.

"Well, I mean, I can give you a tour if you want, but if you don't —"

"NO! I want a tour with you!" Internally, Belén winced at what was definitely too much enthusiasm.

"Umm, great. Well, let me know when you're free and I can take you out." Belén continued to wonder if this meant she had been asked out. She wondered if a town tour counted as a date or if this was a pity party for a girl who didn't know Long Island.

"We can get dinner at The Longshoreman; it's not in Carel, but it's close. It's right on the water." Belén felt pretty confident that she had just been asked out. Remembering his halo of golden hair, she did continue to doubt his interest as charity.

"Well, here's my phone number. Give me a call when you want to show me around."

"How about tonight? It's Friday, and they've got live music. I think you'll definitely like it."

"Yes, that would be great!"

"Your roommate won't mind?" Belén gave herself a slap upside the head mentally as she forgot about her fake roommate and her dying grandmother. She hoped she would not appear callous.

"I'm sure she'll be fine. She mostly sleeps on Friday evenings."

Part 5 | Act I 177

# SAM DESMOND

"Well, that's good luck for me then." The Gatsby smile he gave her put her in a spell of ecstasy.

"Should I wear anything specific?"

"It's pretty casual. I'm sure you'll look beautiful no matter what you decide to wear." Belén wanted to revel in the compliment about her appearance but fought her doubts that he was just trying to be nice.

"Are you going to drink your beer?"

"Ummm... No, I have to drive." Belén tried to pull back the words. Why would she be driving when she was staying with her roommate's family? Patrick looked confused, too. "I mean, my friend is coming later, so she won't be able to pick me up, so her parents left me the car to drive home." Belén gave a ridiculously wide smile.

"Oh...ok."

The next forty minutes were filled with great conversation about music and funny stories. Patrick was a big fan of Nirvana, one of the bands Belén had envisioned her beau ideal to play on his CD player. He came from a large family that was stationed all over Carel and had been for generations. Patrick's father had run the campaign for the current county executive of Suffolk, a position akin to a mayor from what Belén could glean, and currently held the highest political appointee position as a thank-you for the work on the campaign. There was a bit of a Kennedy-esque glamour to his family, and Belén couldn't stop envisioning herself wearing all red with a pill-box hat (not pink because that would be distasteful).

The conductor announced Deer Park as the next stop.

"Well, that's me."

# In the Light of Men

Patrick stood up, and Belén swooned at the chivalry. "It's not you, it's just where you're staying right now." Belén turned around and gave him one last smile. She couldn't believe she had finally met him on the Long Island Rail Road, of all places.

The reality began to set in that she was going on a date with a dreamboat and her ebullience turned into a knot of apprehension. How would she continue her fake life? Would he be able to tell it was a fake life? Why did she need a fake life in the first place? What the hell was she going to wear?

As soon as she ran into the Levittown-style split-ranch built in the '60s she called home, Belén ran to her room and began pulling out of all her clothes, categorizing them as WASPy, borderline WASPy, and ethnic. Thankfully, her "ethnic" pile was filled with mostly gym-type clothes that would never be worn outside of a track. She settled on a boat-neck black top, a knee-length khaki skirt, and plain, black kitten heels with a tortoise-shell button on the side of the shoe. She had no idea how Patrick would dress, but she had hoped to see him in a collared shirt with a cable-knit sweater and khakis. Khakis, the color of the flag of WASPdom. Belén had even taken the step to enhance her makeup strategies. She had just purchased a heated eyelash curler from Sephora following makeup guru Bobbi Brown's advice that "ethnic" lashes did not have a natural curl but could be fixed with one of these contraptions.

Belén read the instructions fairly well, albeit with a distracted mind, and flipped the switch to activate the

SAM DESMOND

heating coils of the mascara-tube-sized contraption. She kept her eyes wide open as well as her mouth and clamped the curler onto her inadequate lashes.

"AAAAAAAHHHHH!!!!!!" For a few seconds she was blinded and had to grope for the table to set down the torture device. With one very agitated eye and another fearing the same fate, she assessed the damage. It looked like a black eye. Her cell phone rang.

"Hey, Claire, I'm on my way. I should be there in about five minutes?"

"That's great," she managed to blurt out as she continued to wince in pain.

"You don't sound well. Are you alright?"

"Yes, just had a mishap with a miniature curling iron."

"That sounds awful! Are you ok?"

"I'll be fine, just don't be alarmed when you see me."

"Ok...see you soon..."

Wonderful, Belén thought, her first date and she had a black eye. She began feeling short of breath, wondering what else could go wrong.

"Anong time dadating itong ka date mo?" Belén's mother asked when her date was coming in her mash-up of native tongue and assimilated English. She was hoping to hide her from Patrick before he noticed the ethnic resemblance between them.

"Soon! Don't answer the door!"

"At bakit wag?" Or "why not" in civilized people's speech.

"Just don't!" Her mother was supposed to be having

## In the Light of Men

dinner somewhere fabulous while discussing charity benefits for the California condor, not sitting at home forcing her siblings to do extra-credit homework.

Belén finished getting dressed and tried to style her hair to cover her affected eye. She kissed her wall of celebrity blonds goodbye for the evening and ran down the stairs.

"Dapat makilala ko muna ang lalaking ito." Her mother demanded to meet the young man to whom she was entrusting the care of her daughter for the evening.

"No, you don't need to meet him. I'd rather you not ruin it!"

The doorbell rang, and Belén squeezed herself outside. Patrick was dressed exactly how she pictured him, right down to the Cole Haan shoes.

"Shouldn't I say hello to your roommate's mom?"

"No, don't worry, she doesn't speak English."

"I can still say hello—-"

"She doesn't like white people."

"Oh...ok."

They walked over to Patrick's car. To Belén's surprise, it was an old Jeep Wrangler, but in a tasteful hunter green. Patrick let her into the passenger seat and drove her away from the land of guido machismo to what she hoped was a storybook village of people just like him. People who would never accept her, but at least she could concede as of better, settler stock.

"I think you'll really like this place. I'm sure you have plenty of places in the city, but nothing is like being on the bay."

Part 5 | Act I 181

SAM DESMOND

"I have a few favorites, like the Russian Tea Room, Smith and Wollensky—"

"Well, no one will have fish as fresh as this place. That's the best part of living on Long Island."

"I wouldn't know. Being a city girl and all."

"Well, lucky you've got me to show you." He flashed that "smile gazing upon the world," and she decided she would love to give him her virginity that night. Although she had read that virginity was a middle-class virtue and mocked by upper-class WASPs. "I think your eye looks okay, from what I can see."

"Really? Thanks, I was pretty worried about it."

"You have gorgeous eyes to begin with. Why do something where you have to hide them?"

"I read that long, curly lashes were important to men."

"According to some chick magazine? It's better you be natural, Claire."

It was everything she wanted to hear for so long, coming from the type of person she longed to hear it from. But it was all being said to someone who was a lie, as much as she enjoyed being Claire.

"So, tell me about your major?"

"Well, I decided on International Marketing because I'm a good writer, but it wouldn't be practical to major in that, so I am going to study marketing in Eastern Europe and eventually join the Peace Corps to help banking develop in the former Soviet satellite countries." Belén took a breath after reciting her carefully prepared speech.

"That sounds amazing, but you don't really sound

## In the Light of Men

too crazy about that plan. It's kind of an afterthought. You said you like writing."

"Well, I'd love to study English literature, but it's not very practical."

"But if it's what you love, then why not?"

"I don't know. I just couldn't do it. I mean, my mother thinks—"

"What do *you* think? It's okay if it's not what your mom thinks."

"I think I'd love to major in English literature."

"So do it! There's nothing stopping you. I'd love to read your work…well, if you'll let me."

Belén couldn't believe how well this was going. He wanted to read her writing, an act of intimacy she was less comfortable about than sex. He thought she should pursue English literature. She wondered who Patrick was and why was he so perfect. She pinched herself—possibly too hard—but couldn't believe someone had come into being seemingly from her demanding imagination.

"You seem very genuine, Claire. You shouldn't hide behind other people's ideas just because you think that'll make them happy."

When they arrived at the restaurant, Patrick put his arm around her, and she had to remind herself to take in air. They were seated at a table in full view of the water and the moonlight. The other patrons looked like they could have been Patrick's family, but Belén was surprised at the hokey, nautical décor of the place. It reminded her of a homemade Red Lobster.

Part 5 | Act I 183

SAM DESMOND

"Welcome to The Longshoreman. Can I get you something to drink?"

"I'll take a gin and tonic," Patrick replied.

"I'll have a Sprite."

"Claire, they don't care that you're underage. Just pretend you're in the city."

"No, it's okay. I'll have a Sprite."

Patrick laughed and turned to the incredulous waitress. "I'll stick with my gin and tonic."

"Sorry, I don't feel comfortable drinking. My mom would—"

"But she's not here." He gave a devilishly sexy half-smile and added, "but I would like to meet her someday."

"Well, maybe one of these days."

"What's she like?"

"She's pretty much a lady of leisure. She doesn't spend too much time in New York. She likes to travel to Europe a lot."

"She sounds like someone who would love to have her daughter study English literature or art history."

"Yes, you would think that."

"There are these amazing seafood skins here—"

Suddenly, a nasal, piercing Long Island accent screamed, "OH MY GOD!!! I can't believe you're here, too!!" The screeching severed Belén's spine and Patrick politely smiled. In horror, Belén saw a high school acquaintance and stared back with her mouth agape.

"How are you doing?" Belén managed to compose herself and appear courteous.

"I'm fucking GREAT! Isn't it awesome to be done

184     Part 5  |  Act i

# In the Light of Men

with 'Queer' Park High School?! Yo, I don't know who you are, guy," the unwelcome classmate said turning towards Patrick, "but you got one smart bitch here."

"Claire, do you want to introduce me?" asked Patrick, somewhat uncomfortable.

"Why the fuck's he calling you 'Claire'?"

# SECOND ACT

Part 5 | Act 2     187

# HOLY MOTHER

Years went by and I answered
   "yes" to every request

She pretended I existed only in the form she wanted;
   part of the family, no explanation
   not her glaring mistake

I didn't want to tell the world of her past
   but she never left me with a choice

I'm not sorry for her anymore
I won't grin it all away
For once she can't convince me it was my fault

The manipulation of extended gestation
   makes for a breach birth
We never know maternal motivation
   past the drying of the teat
Some of us suckle barren globs,
    Others, hemlock of our future aspirations

When the burial occurs, am I to say "I'm sorry" once again?
No, I'd rather waste my Catholic guilt
   on holy mothers
   made of stone

Part 5 | Act 3

PATRICK'S MOST DEVOTEDLY IRISH-CATHOLIC aunt, Aunt Aisling, his father's older sister, was in favor of her having an abortion. Had the doctor performed the tubal ligation when she first requested it at nineteen, all this heartache could have been avoided. Patrick's stepmother was the only person who was willing to give her the false Catholic dogma that God would ensure their unplanned baby would be malady-free.

Patrick tried his best to comfort her, but he was embroiled in his own allegiance to eugenics to offer any real sympathy. At least they weren't infertile. They had always secretly judged couples with failed in vitro attempts—if God and science both said no, wasn't that a clear sign that you weren't meant to continue your genes? But here they were, pregnant after ten years of marriage and homeowners, because of a false belief that he didn't need to pull out anymore because "I can't be that good at pulling out. One of us has to be infertile."

He had come in her twice, and she was pregnant.

All of her medications were Class C—enough to worry about having a special-needs child but not enough to make it definite. But could she even handle the withdrawal from the meds *and* pregnancy hormones? Was it certain

Part 5 | Act 3      193

SAM DESMOND

suicide? Filicide with her risk of post-partum psychosis? She was certain of post-partum depression as a best bet.

Gestational diabetes was also a concern, given the obesity. That one nurse they saw judged her harshly on her question about obesity affecting fetal development; masturbatorily stroking her cross necklace, she said, "Your weight should never be a factor in whether to continue a pregnancy." Oddly, whereas the 40-pound weight gain of pregnancy had terrified her eating-dis-ordered youth, gaining 150 pounds on medication had brought her through the physical transformation into womanhood of losing her beauty and no longer feared pregnancy pounds. She lost half of the medication weight and didn't want to be near 300 pounds again. But she'd have "baby on board" this time. She'd be a pregnant fat, a more acceptable fat. "No one can yell at you for being fat when you're pregnant," Blair had told her. Even though her generation's brand of feminism said you had to transform into a MILF after motherhood.

What about her vagina? Google didn't even have real, flesh photos of an episiotomy vagina/anus, just ghastly stories of how to never be able to please a man again. The lover she had last year had told her, "Yes, it's very different after kids. It's much wider. Why do you think anal has become so popular?" She had always been told she was extraordinarily small, or perhaps that was an ethnic expectation white guys had of her. But that was a literal loss of maidenhood she couldn't han-dle. Blair had said, while pumping breast milk in the bathroom at a wedding, that she opted for a Caesarean

## In the Light of Men

to "avoid incontinence. No one talks about it, but it's a big problem."

Patrick was lovingly fine with a looser, pee-leaking vagina. Half because of fetish, half because he was always a perfect, understanding Gen-X dreamboat who, as a lover, could be characterized by, "No, no. Don't blow me. I'll get hard eating you out." She had joked with Chaim that her husband, as a gay lover, would "be neither top nor bottom, but whatever his partner needed in the moment." Chaim said, "No, Johnny football hero would be expected to be a top."

Her husband would be a great dad. He was a great father to her. She'd be a shit mom. Just like Patrick's mother. She'd fall into a depression, and the child would lay in its filth for days like Patrick had as a baby until his grandmother rescued him for preservation of social standing.

But Patrick's other aunt, Aunt Aoife, his father's younger sister, assured her that no such thing would happen. She would be there to watch the baby if she fell into a depression. This was going to be another test of character she would fail. And what would the child look like? She had told her husband she would only want a child if they could clone him. What if the baby got her dark hair, her short stature? What if it was a girl, and she inherited both their broad shoulders? They would have to push her to be a lesbian. She'd be in therapy—"But I like boys!"

As long as the child was smart. Patrick could never handle a special-needs child. Or a retarded special-needs

## SAM DESMOND

child. He always saw things optimized, efficient. They would grow apart, he, resentful, and they would get divorced, bringing a child into the world they both knew should have been euthanized for its inability to survive or thrive on its own.

She wanted to be stupid for once. Believe in God. Believe it would be okay. Believe she could keep this baby. Why couldn't she be a typical, stupid woman who prayed when action was needed, who believed in star signs, who was blissfully childlike at the thought of harsh responsibility? Her husband clasped her hand as his aunt reached out.

"Dear, this is for your well-being. The Catholic Church's stance on abortion is clear when it comes to preserving the health of the mother," said Aunt Aisling.

Dear Mommy,

We hope you're feeling better today! Yesterday was really scary for us. You were screaming so much, and Tyrconnell and I thought we were being bad, but we were trying so hard to be good. We didn't move at all and stayed right next to you on the couch all day because we know it makes you feel better to hold us. Every time you cried, we made sure to lick away your tears so they wouldn't stay on your beautiful face. They're really salty, your tears, but we love salty snacks! It was good we had those snacks because when you're like this, we have to wait for Daddy to come home to get food in our bowls. Don't let this make you sadder! We can wait for our food, the mini meatloaves you baked for us are so good that we can wait all day for them. We're so lucky to have a mommy who cooks for us. Everyone at the park says they only get kibble, but we get organic people food! Can we have more meat than brown rice for the next time you make us meatloaves?

Mommy, please just try to stop yelling, especially at Daddy. He always tells us how much he loves you more than anything in the world. Even whiskey! And we know how much he loves whiskey because we're both named after whiskeys. When you yell, we get so scared and just want to hide. I know I'm too big to hide under the couch like I used to when I first came home, but it's the only place I feel safe when you're so mad. You and Daddy always tell us it's not our fault when you're yelling, but

## SAM DESMOND

we're always worried we're doing something wrong. We stopped chewing your shoes, and we only chew the furniture when you and Daddy have been gone for too long. What else can we do? We really miss going on all those walks down to the bay at night with you and Daddy because there are so many new smells! We love our backyard, but we know everything out there. And we keep smelling Midnight even though she's under the dirt.

I know you and Daddy get mad at Tyrconnell when he sneaks out of the backyard through the hole in the fence and goes to the neighbor's house—I tell him every time not to—but he likes the people there. They don't yell, and they always play with him outside. Tyrconnell was older when you became his mommy and daddy, so he thinks he can have another mommy and daddy, but I don't know any other mommy or daddy but you guys. And I love you so much. I get so mad at myself that I can only make you happy, but I can't keep you happy. I can't be happy even when you're okay because I know you'll be sad soon. I know you love me so much that it hurts you because it makes you think of how sad you'll be when I die. Is that why you ignore me sometimes? So you won't love me as much, and then it won't hurt when I die? I don't want to die. I try not to get sick because I remember how scared Daddy got when he thought I hurt my leg playing at the dog park. I promise I'll live as long as I can so you don't kill yourself when I die like you promised Daddy you would. I know you think cloning me will save you from the pain, but I don't know how to come back to you and Daddy after I die.

## In the Light of Men

I wish you could believe in the Rainbow Bridge so you could feel less worried about the future and just enjoy the time Tyrconnell and I are here.

Sometimes other doggies tell me how much better their mommies are than you are because their mommies never forget to feed them or take them out for walks, but I tell them I have the best mommy in the world! You love doggies so much and feel like we should be treated like children. I know your brain hurts you and that's why we don't know how you'll be for the day. You even keyed that woman's fancy car when she almost ran us over and didn't apologize!

We hate it so much when we're not with you, but if you're on the treadmill downstairs (we're scared of the basement!) or leaving the house, we know that you're feeling better. Please, Mommy, just remember we love you so much. You and Daddy are our whole world, and when you're not well, we can't be okay.

Your loyal dog,
Morangie

# FOURTH ACT

Part 5 | Act 4

THE ROLE OF THE MISTRESS—GLAMOROUS, PAS-sionate, forbidden—was intrinsically romantic to her because even the most innocent, simple communication was made exciting and tragically fleeting. A lust-filled gaze turned into a casual nod of 'hello.' A naughty emoji in a text sporting exaggerated whore-red puckered lips. A lingering embrace with hands closely guarded north of the Mason-Dixon line.

She had forever admired the "drippingly" sexy, aloof mistress in cinema and literature along with the otherwise honorable, diligent, and devoted husbands/ fathers who couldn't help themselves in the coquettish touch but iron fist of a femme fatale. It was feminine allure to the furthest exultation. She had longed to be covered in rose petals in the masturbatory fantasy of a Lester Burnham. Or, as a haughtier reference, the Di-doian kink in the well-laid, globally impactful plans of Aeneas. She chose not to see the seedier, debased side of men who were serial "cheaters." Instead, she venerated the deep friendship of an affair that could grow without the mundane entanglements of mortgages, laundry, and child-rearing. She wanted to be a breath of fresh air to an otherwise dutiful good man who gasped to take it in.

SAM DESMOND

Never considered a traditional beauty, she loved feeling like she was giving the middle finger to the conventional wife/mother who pathetically believed her aging skin and sagging tits could compete with the nubile twenty-somethings that would always be around. No, she didn't believe any woman could possess a man fully and show her mortality.

In her adolescent, high school fantasies, she dreamed of being a metropolitan co-ed marrying Patrick Bateman, the consummate gentleman and bedroom misogynist, who would, of course, 'cheat' on her but continue to be loyal in public face. That's what a good marriage was: the ultimate political ally who defended you to the death, but only when the public watched. With a European marriage, she (and Patrick) could play the conformist darlings and toy with affairs to bolster their self-esteem.

Patrick was nothing like Patrick Bateman. Instead, he was devoted, understanding, and despite their mutual agreement and delight at an "open" marriage, never really took full advantage of it. Despite her self-throat-slitting reassurances to others that "...he can fuck some 22-year-old hottie. He's prime dick, he deserves it! He can brag to me later about how she tasted like peaches and cream...," it was really just poor bargaining for his social respect. Throughout courtship and matrimony, he flirted with other women in her presence—cashiers, waitresses, good friends, frenemies, co-workers—much to her immediate chagrin and latent rage. She could see others 'feeling sorry' for her, and nothing could be more detrimental than pity for someone who longed to

## In the Light of Men

be envied. She constantly told him, "…let the waitress blow you when you go to the bathroom, not while I'm asking for more bread." But he knew the blatant, disrespectful flirting was the one thing she couldn't be 'cool' enough to tolerate.

In her solitude, she sat on the ocean side of the island, admiring the moon's ability to exploit another's light.

Much like she did with her writing.

She had always known that her death would be by her own hand. After her first experience plummeting into the abyss, she lived every moment of happiness as a countdown to when the darkness would cloak her again. Patrick knew her writings would be his responsibility to share following her inevitable suicide. She knew he would be devastated but relieved of the pressure and the patience to keep her functional. He was her guardian angel who clipped his wings to be in the trenches with her, and despite being overwhelmed with love and gratitude, she only gave him her worst. She always knew the best she could do for him was release him of the malady of loving her. It was the only suicide letter, even in her greatest splendors of terrifying mania, she could not write. He could see through her bullshit and still wanted to be with her despite the ugliness that remained (or revealed itself) once her charms were called out.

All the years they were together, she spent abusing him to force him away from her. But he never left. He fought her dragons and trained her to fight them on her own. But the darkness always won and he didn't need a bullshit letter deifying him. She wouldn't insult him

## SAM DESMOND

with that now. Besides, Woolf had already outwritten her decades ago, and even her suicide was disgustingly derivative of a master's. Instead, she sealed a poem she had written years ago during her last depression that had been the closest she came to capturing her love for him.

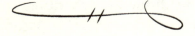

*In the Light of Men*

# "THE UNWILLING PATRON"

How do you stand by me, through all the trials I give you?
Can you ever forgive me for all the roles I've made you play?
    The Father
    The Lover
    The Savior
You handle the carousel of therapy
    with such grace, I can barely
    genuflect in your wake
I don't deserve the breath you
    waste on bringing me back
    to existence
But you always bring your generosity,
    cutting all the warranties I dread
Thank you for the patience I haven't
    earned
Thank you for the love I never
    imagined
Thank you for the halo that you wear
    so unconsciously
If ever I do pull myself together,
    you'll be the first to reap the benefits
But you'll be the last to piece it whole,
    for all I've ever given you are
    shambles of the monument
I've built.

All my love,
Belén

Part 5 | Act 4    207

# SAM DESMOND

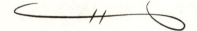

She placed a rock on top of her letter to Patrick and turned her attention to the cinderblocks, rope, and Gorilla duct tape she had also brought with her on the ferry to Fire Island. She slithered the rope through a cinderblock and made knots to secure it. Then she knotted and wrapped the rope on her leg and used three rolls of duct tape to keep the rope from slipping off her once she was in the ocean. She repeated the procedure with her other leg.

The madness had returned, and she could no longer torture the one and only man (person, really) who saw her as gorgeous when both her internal and external lights had failed to come on. She lay back on the sand and looked up at the beaming moon. Charlatan, she thought, you're a con artist fooling everyone for millennia that you have any worth beyond what you rip off from the sun.

A photobox, labeled "Open in Case of Suicidal Ideations," was next to her final letters. Inside were pictures of their life together, their wonderful dogs and cats who had passed, inscriptions in journals he bought for her, and years of birthday, Valentines, and anniversary cards from him. She read her favorite note from her husband one last time:

"...May we always continue to build a stronger and fruitful life together. Thank you for changing and letting yourself experience joy and bring happiness to our lives. I love you, babe!"

# In the Light of Men

She stood and picked up the cinder blocks, staring out into the moonlit ocean to join her monster, muse, and mentor.

# FIFTH ACT

Part 5 | Act 5

# MENTAL HEALTH
*Advocacy*

# I DIED AT 27
BY BELÉN STRATTON-DELANEY

B eing a creative type and having an inkling that mental illness was in my future following an abnormal psychology class in high school, I hoped to become a l'enfant terrible of the literary world and die tragically at the age of twenty-seven like Kurt Cobain.

Perhaps it was my dual Irish/Filipino Catholic upbringing or low threshold for physical pain, but suicide was not my preferred option. I had even begun to list "cool ways to die." My favorite was a fantasy where, as a wealthy, eccentric writer who obtained her pilot's license, I would be caught in a raging storm and come crashing into the Atlantic.

In this quasi-self-fulfilling prophecy, I did "die" at twenty-seven and remained in purgatory until I was almost forty. There had always been something "off" about me. Teachers, classmates, parents, and friends always gave this puzzled stare when I answered routine questions like, "how are you?" with "I would like to be happy, but that's boring, so I'd like to think about people who are dead or suffering."

Anything I was interested in had to be pursued to the extreme, and in a short period of time before my curiosity waned, I could only watch movies I had already seen because I would not need to concentrate on the plotline.

Once I started working, my shopping sprees became epic. As a sixteen-year-old, I managed to open fourteen (14) credit cards at the Walt Whitman Mall and maxed out each one multiple times before I was eighteen. When I had my first real, corporate job in midtown Manhattan, I would spend $300 to $500 a lunch hour at the stores surrounding my Madison Avenue office. The rationalization I provided to my husband (whose wages funded these manic episodes) was that I never paid full price, so I was, in fact, saving him money.

Following eight years of explosive, violent (with the physical aggression coming unprovoked from me) arguments, my husband pleaded with me to seek professional help. The social worker I went to see referred me to a psychiatrist within the first two minutes of our session citing, "clearly there's something chemical going on with you." The psychiatrist, with her posh, upper east side office and waiting room filled with ladies of leisure who lunch, diagnosed me with bipolar disorder and ADHD in fifteen minutes and prescribed a slew of medications. In six months, the dosage for the most potent medication had septupled from the initial prescription.

Within a year, I had gained 150 pounds (going from a size 4/6 to a 3X being tight), lost two jobs, and spoke only to my husband. Incoherently, most of the time. Blaming the medication for making me too tired to workout like I used to and crave carbs, I "weaned" myself off psychotropic medications in one week. The depression that hit felt like the payment for my lifetime of mania. Rapidly, I unleashed racing thoughts on all my insecurities: being morbidly obese, being too ethnic looking, not going to an Ivy League, losing valedictorian by .001, not breaking 1400 on my SATs because I was too lazy to take a prep course. Not only was I a fat loser now, but it turned out I had never actually been a winner.

This was my rock bottom. I slept twenty of twenty-four hours. I was so overweight I could not even walk the stairs from our bedroom to the bathroom.

Instead, I had a Guinness pint glass next to our bed that I would urinate into and empty out the window into our backyard. All I wanted to eat was fast food. In one sitting, I could scarf down a Wendy's triple cheeseburger, large fries, bacon and cheese baked potato, twelve chicken nuggets, and a large vanilla frosty. This would all be washed down with a large orange soda.

Desperately in the throes of suicidal ideation (I was still too lazy and insecure to literally pull the trigger myself), all I wished for was to die of a massive heart attack. My fear was that it would be a paralyzing stroke instead, and I would be forced to live forever as a vegetable trapped in my own torturing thoughts.

I began seeing a new psychiatrist on Long Island who I told, "I feel like the person I used to be, the one I could at least pretend was impressive, is dead, and I'm the pitiful replacement. Everyone who supposedly cares about me only wants her back. What's the point of living?" In nine months I would have two involuntary psychiatric hospitalizations.

Being defeated by my own thoughts for nearly my entire life, I had no choice but to listen to ideas that did not develop in my own mind. I learned to let go of my preoccupation with assuming what awful, judgmental thoughts people had of me and started to just be honest about what I could and could not do at that point. Once I was unscripted with my friends and family, I was pleasantly surprised to hear that they were not mourning the loss of my old self but that they believed I was still talented and intelligent despite where I was at the moment. Many people also told me what they missed about me had nothing to do with my size or the CV I had, but the sense of humor and thoughtfulness that had come to characterize me in their minds. One of our closest friends confided that he constantly re-read a thank-you note I had sent years ago because no one had ever believed in him that much.

Finally, I've embraced my quirks, oddities, strong but fleeting passion, and abilities as part of who I am. Whether those qualities stem from being bipolar is irrelevant now because I am not compartmentalized. The old Belén, trapped in a constant state of frenzied insecurity, died at twenty-seven. She did not die as the famous writer I had hoped she would

## In the Light of Men

become but as a young woman whose existence was too mired in false perceptions of others to continue into adulthood. I am still getting used to the new Belén, and she is as awkward as any adolescent, but I know she has one very impressive trait: potential for longevity.

# FINAL ACT

2024

Part 5 | Final Act    219

BELÉN POSTED A PHOTO OF HER AND PATRICK laughing and completely content in each other's eyes on Facebook with the caption:

"As I get older (bewildered at how I'm going to be 40 in less than 6 months), I notice I look at older photos of myself with a kinder eye...

Or maybe, I've finally learned to approach myself the way I do most stories—focus on the good in addition to acknowledging the bad—

While in the past all I would've noticed in this photo was a gaping double chin, today, when it flashed on my TV, I noticed the great smiles, affection, and humor between me and the man I've loved for over 20 years that was all still there, even with an additional 100 pounds."

She sat on the couch, nestled in Patrick's shoulder nook with their dogs, Morangie and Tyrconnell, lying on their laps and smiled at the pure contentment she had.

# About the Author

AWARD-WINNING JOURNALIST SAM DESMOND IS currently the Contributing Editor for *The Suffolk County News*, which covers the southeastern portion of Islip Town on Long Island.

Previously, her essay "The Gift of the Tortured Specter" on Joan Vollmer was included in the anthology, "Fever Spores: The Queer Reclamation of William S. Burroughs" published by Rebel Satori Press in 2022.

She lives in Bayport in her aptly named Squirrel Cottage with her husband of over 20 years, their 2 dogs, and 4 cats.